SQUARED AWAY

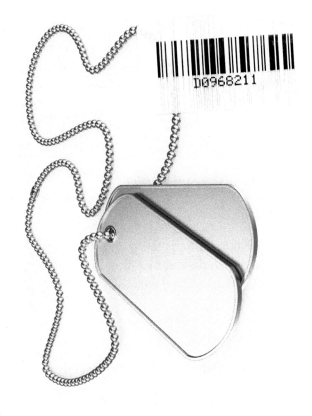

Alicia Dill

White Bird Publications
P.O. Box 90145
Austin, Texas 78709
http://www.whitebirdpublications.com

Copyright©2019—Alicia Dill
Cover design: Molly Phipps—We've Got You Covered Book Design

ISBN: 978-1-63363-384-1
LCCN: 2019935198

PRINTED IN THE UNITED STATES OF AMERICA

This book is dedicated to those in harm's way.
Your service and sacrifice are a solid foundation
to build a life on. Remember to live it!

Acknowledgments

In my journey, a few people carried me through as a published author. My significant other, Tony who never let me give up. He is my first editor and persistence coach. My grandma, Betty, the artist who gave me inspiration into how real life works and taught me how to turn it into beautiful things.

This took a talented team. My editor, Latoya C. Smith with LCSLiterary.com who understood my vision and made this book worth reading. For Molly Phipps (wegotyoucoveredbookdesign@gmail.com) who brought my book to life with cover and website design. For Evelyn and the whole White Bird Publications' team for making my dream a reality. For Jessie Glenn, Katie Fairchild and the Mindbuck Media team who encouraged me to get out there. For Deborah Jayne with all her many talents.

SQUARED AWAY

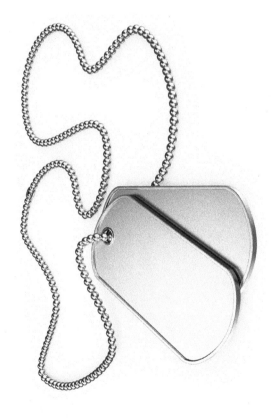

White Bird
Publications

Prologue

September 7, 2007

"What am I doing here?" I whispered, but saying the words aloud didn't give me any further insight.

The seconds ticked by. The hourglass of my life sifted away from me, one grain of sand at a time. Being deployed in one of the most dangerous places on planet Earth, I considered my mortality far too often. How long did I have left? How would I spend it? Two questions a twenty-six-year-old should not be asking.

It was my last guard duty, on my last deployment. Military life was not for me. After six years serving, I knew it, and the Army knew it. When I had explained my job as a military journalist to my family, it had all sounded so much more exciting than it turned out to be. I couldn't stomach the idea of another year of soldiering. Being assigned to guard duty instead of working on the camp magazine was like sticking a fork in me—I was done. Instead of writing stories and using my degree, I was trying not to fall asleep on my M16. It was loaded, after all. Sure, the money was great, but as an investment in my own sanity, I was getting out.

"McCoy, it's quitting time, you lucky..." The voice of Private First Class Jacob Glass trailed off as he yelled up the steps of the guard tower. He thankfully stopped himself before he said something degrading. This was the new world order where educated, empowered women were also stuck on watch.

I briefed Glass on the day's inactivity and cleared my weapon in a nearby container. I packed my gear in the small pockets of my Camelbak and headed down the ancient steps of the station. No one had to tell me twice.

As I walked to the dining facility, I tried to make my meal options sound appealing. A hot meal was never a possibility when working a shift that ended just before midnight. The second shift guards received bottom-of-the-barrel leftovers after the local cooks stopped serving at eight p.m. My only hope was for a stocked salad bar and a peanut butter and jelly sandwich.

After I assembled a chicken salad for dinner, I added the sun-dried tomato salad dressing my little sister had sent me from home. I was a foodie at heart. I valued my slim hips, so I had to be creative with my meals.

I grabbed a Styrofoam container at the beginning of the line and took my dinner to go.

On the walk to my room, I took a good look around. The way the endless black sky continued was beautiful. I thought about my family far away. I considered my grandma smoking her nightly cigarette on the porch in her southern Missouri home. They were under this sky, too, in some other time.

As I entered the cramped living quarters, I saw my roommate and best friend of six years, Sergeant Concepcion Chapa. I owed her my life literally and figuratively after an amateur move on my part. It had happened when we were running near the base; she ran ahead and tripped me. I fell to my knees, and she pulled my T-shirt, dragging me back toward her. I pulled my headphones out, "Why'd you trip me?"

She pointed ahead on the path where a horned viper head peeked out while its body was burrowed under the sand. With a combat boot, snakes were less threatening, but with tennis shoes and bare calves, hemorrhagic bleeding wasn't how I wanted to go out. I never let her run ahead again.

She was watching a pirated copy of one of the latest popular movies back in the States. With her headphones on, she didn't hear me come in. I set my food down and jumped on the bed, where her tiny frame was sprawled out in front of my MacBook Pro.

"Dammit, McCoy, you ruined the sexy mood I was creating in my head. This is the best part," she said.

A very naked eighteen-year-old muscular man was having fake sex with a plastic surgeon's golden ticket, a forty-something blonde cougar.

"Monkey puke, monkey puke," I lifted her earphones off her head. The phrase *monkey puke* was something my dad sang when the brief sex scenes of movies raced by my young eyes. He was too lazy to fast-forward, and movie night was too sacred of a time to put my sisters and me to bed early. I later decided this was the reason I became shy during all nude and kissing scenes. Concepcion knew about my aversion to nudity and used it against me whenever possible.

After I riled my battle buddy, I walked to the communal bathroom to get ready for the night. Searching the mirror, I smiled at my reflection, an old habit for applying makeup. At five feet nine inches, I was taller than many other female soldiers, but less elegant or sophisticated than the rest of the women in my family. Instead of waif-thin, I was lean and athletic, my coffee-colored long hair pulled back, making my features look harsh in the halogen lights. I considered how soon it would be until I would be able to wear my hair down for good. The strands were breaking off after being in a tight bun throughout the years.

I examined my pores up close and thanked my expensive and rigorous skin-care regimen. My time there was showing on my face, and no amount of miracle cream could fix my sunken eyes perpetually looking tired. They were supposed to be my best feature, according to Concepcion. They changed in intensity, from shades of green to hazel, as often as my mood. As a Gemini, I was a different person depending on the day. I would pay for these years of stress on my body.

I heard the door of the bathroom open and close while I had my face pressed up to the mirror. In another world, I would be able to obsess in private, but not in the Army. Before I could see who it was, a hand slapped my toweled behind. Concepcion. Payback was sooner than I imagined.

"Get out of your head, girl. You'll get another migraine."

I turned around and shook my head. I didn't respond. What she said was true. My migraine diagnosis was another check in the "con" category for staying in the service.

I listened as the water turned on. I hoped Concepcion hadn't moved my stuff away from the good shower. I needed hot water to release some of the tension in my shoulders from holding up a gun all day. The good shower meant temperature control was possible. I looked in the mirror to see her taking the shower next to mine. Good girl.

"Are you ready to be out of this sandbox?" The noise of the shower between us. "Can I get a *hell yeah*, Sergeant?"

"What are you saying?" She didn't hear me.

Showers here were mostly private, but I was feeling giddy about leaving this place. As much as I bitched, we were lucky we had running water. It was worse in Afghanistan.

Concepcion sang out louder so I could hear. She did a great Cher impression, and I could tell she was also in a good mood for our last night.

I peeked outside the shower stall to see if anyone else had come in since I'd entered. I wasn't ready to entertain the whole camp.

I screamed out the next verse while I rubbed some

remaining sand into my skin, exfoliating the sweat as best I could. Her energy was infectious. She was as excited as I was to get back home. I was going to miss our Cher-in-the-shower time.

Concepcion's voice was stronger than mine, but that was okay with me. My stomach dropped a bit when I considered leaving her at the airport. Like the Army, she was a constant in my life. She'd saved me from myself more than a few times. I was going to miss my friend.

Chapter One

July 20, 2009

I wriggled underneath my Egyptian cotton sheets. Why couldn't I sleep when I was this tired? I stretched my arms and legs in the queen-size bed, willing my muscles to relax. Every little noise in the old farmhouse grew louder. The crickets singing outside my window usually were pleasant summer sounds, but I was getting pissed off at them rubbing their legs together furiously.

I glanced at my alarm clock and read the time: 3:32 a.m. Another partial repose. As if on cue, my cell phone near my bed beeped, alerting me I had a voicemail. When had the phone gone off? I must have blocked it out somehow.

After punching in my voicemail password, I heard a robot voice telling me the number. It seemed to endlessly drone on. It wasn't a real number. The voice was accented but familiar somehow.

"It's Blake…you know, Hamdani, 155th for life. I got your number from one of the guys here. I'm calling about Chapa. I need to talk. Can you just check on her for me? Take care, bye."

I pushed play again. The second time didn't make a difference. His voice was cryptic, and his repeat of our unit's "open sesame" password had a fragility to it.

I scrolled through my contacts and dialed Chapa's cell. After ten rings, a robot voice told me no voicemail was available for this number. I called again. Nothing. Not surprised. When Chapa had made the transition from military to FBI, her job took her away for long stretches of time. I missed talking to her every day, but two years after we both left the military, we would call every few weeks and usually talk for three straight hours until one of us had to call time. It was all about quality time over quantity for our friendship. The last time we had spoken was over a month ago now, when she was getting a pedicure, and I was complaining at the hardware store about how fast my deployment savings were disappearing under the weight of owning an old house that needed lots of repairs.

"You should move to Miami and take over my condo when I'm away. It's small, but it's Miami, girl! Think of the men!"

"Yeah, right," I said. "Miami is too cool for school. That's your town. I'm pretty sure the men are like the men everywhere. They want us to be all things to all people. I don't need someone to take care of besides myself."

I lay back down on the bed and tried to relax. "Hamdani. Hamdani." I whispered the word in a trance. Familiar but not. I was almost back to sleep when I remembered Chapa used Skype to stay in touch with our former Iraqi translator. That was his name.

I sat up on the bed and wrapped myself in the duvet. I walked to the kitchen and booted up my laptop. A coyote howled in the distance. It was too early for this shit. But for her, I would call this guy. Only for her.

I waited as the circle of connection went around in sky blue circles. It had been at least a year since I'd signed on last. Concepcion Chapa was offline. Her status photo was set to a sexualized avatar of herself. Dark curled hair, almond-shaped eyes, and a red lip. Her avatar even carried her signature bucket accessory purse. Really. I laughed hard on an empty stomach. This ruthless warrior was now a cartoon lady.

I found the contact search page and typed in Hamdani, and 731 names appeared. I typed in *Blake* before the Hamdani. Only twenty-three were listed. Blake wasn't even his real first name. Most translators working for the US military used pseudonyms to make it easier for the soldiers. Blake was more comfortable for an American to yell in a firefight than Uday or Qusay. Semantics.

I scrolled through and noticed one of the contacts was still online. Could it be this easy?

His profile said he was twenty-five, living in Jordan. Maybe.

My own avatar was the standard Skype outline of a person with no frills. Fine by me.

I turned off my webcam and dialed the number. *Here goes nothing.*

"*Marhaban.*"

"*Marhaban,*" It had been years since I'd attempted that Arabic greeting. "Hello, I am looking for Blake. This is Joelle."

A cough, voices in the background.

"I don't know you. I think you are mistaken. You're American?"

I hesitated. "Yes, I am. I dialed this number after I got a message from Blake Hamdani."

"Thank you. I'm sorry, you have the wrong Blake

Hamdani."

"I apologize, I thought it could be one of my translators. Guess there are twenty-two more of you on here, huh."

"Yes, Blake is a common name in Jordan." Funny. He cleared his throat.

"Okay, thanks. Sorry to bother you."

I hung up and scrolled down the list of the other Blake Hamdanis. None of the others were online.

I enlarged a photo of another younger guy with the same name, and this one had a few numbers at the end. I was pretty sure I had the right one, but he wasn't online. I set my headset on the antique desk. My laptop looked small on the giant surface. Stacks of newspapers were piled up on top of the cords.

I leaned forward and closed my eyes. I couldn't recall a tangible image of Blake. I pictured the elegant, determined, and vibrant Mallika instead. The guys were usually paired with male teams. Concepcion and I were a team with Mallika. Blake was one of the intelligence translators whom Concepcion worked with on the monthly village councils. I was not on those missions. He was younger than us, baby-faced. In the morning hours, he was a blur of small details that didn't help me in finding a random Skype contact.

My headphones shook on the table. The funny

Blake was calling back. I swallowed and stared down. Was it safe for me to answer? I was a civilian now reaching back into a world I had left behind. I pushed the green button.

"Hello?"

"Hello, Sergeant McCoy…this is Hamdani. Your translator? Remember?"

His voice was monotone. Formal. British accent.

"Didn't you just say you didn't know me?"

"Yes, that is true," he said. "There was a man here with an unfriendly face."

"Unfriendly, oh. Where is here?"

"The internet café. I am paying to use the connection."

The voices behind him grew louder. Someone was yelling near the caller.

"Yeah, that makes sense. You called and left me a message?"

"I am sorry I had to bother you. I sincerely apologize. I need to speak to our mutual friend, and she is not available."

That was two apologies so far, first me now him.

"Well, I'm not in touch with her every minute. I tried to call, and she wasn't answering for me, either."

His voice was getting louder as his location buzzed with activity. Another world from here.

"You don't understand. She hasn't answered for several weeks now. This is a serious matter."

"I don't know. We live far apart. You know how far Miami is from St. Louis?"

At the mention of Miami, I closed my eyes and remembered the beach photos that had covered our room on deployment.

"No, I do not." Formal tone again.

I adjusted my headphones. They were squeezing my ears to numbness. I was awake at least. "Why is it serious, Blake? By the way, I'm not a sergeant. I was a specialist."

This distinction of rank was important to me. I wasn't promoted. She was.

"Fine, Specialist. Did you know she was helping me come to your country?"

I shook my head in the dark. "No."

"Did you talk about me?"

"No, I didn't talk to her about you. I'm glad she was helping you, but it has been a while since I spoke to her."

He sighed into the phone. "I'm almost out of credit here. I may be able to get more."

"Well, I will have her call you when she calls me back."

"I need her to call me soon because my interview

14

for my visa is coming up next week."

"Okay, I will have her call you."

"I am running out of minutes. Find her and make her call me. It's not—"

The line cut off. I took off the headset and examined the length of the call. Three minutes and twenty-one seconds. How much did credit cost again? I yawned deeply and hunched my shoulders. A file came through Skype. I opened the PDF after it downloaded, read it, and saved it to my desktop.

Concepcion worked as an FBI agent in Miami. I had come back to my hometown to pursue community journalism greatness. In other words, I was wasting time and money because I wasn't sure what to do next.

The last time we talked, she had to run because her BMW Z4 coupe was ready after getting an oil change at the dealership. I was sweating it out in my old Jeep Cherokee without an air conditioner, waiting on a farmer to meet me for an interview. I wrote articles for my small-town paper, *The Cantonian*. It was a way I could write for a small pittance of thirty thousand dollars a year but not have to push myself out of familiar areas.

I couldn't remember exactly what we said. I tried to focus on the last time I had spoken to her, during her pedicure.

My own upbringing was considerably less interesting. I was from the middle of the Midwest. Growing up in Canton just begged for me to chase every adventure thrown my way. By the time I was eighteen years old, I was ready to run in the worst way. The military appealed to me. I was told I was too much of a free spirit to conform to that type of lifestyle. It took me two enlistments to prove it to myself. It was an instant ego boost for my dad to have a daughter in the Missouri National Guard trained as a journalist and a military police officer. The yellow ribbon bumper sticker and the flag in the yard were the highest forms of currency in farm country.

I had met Concepcion in job training for the military. We became instant friends the same way most people in the military did: we were assigned the same room. My first impression of her the day we met revealed nothing about the problems of her past. She was exotic, petite. Her voice carried for such a small woman. With well-muscled arms from nine weeks of basic training, she was tough to read with her penciled-in eyebrows and lined lips. Features too precise to be a real person. After spending so much time together, I started to wear mascara and tinted ChapStick, something my own mother couldn't get me to do. I wasn't interested in being pretty for anyone else before, but after Chapa convinced me I was enhancing my natural beauty instead of covering it, I agreed.

"If you just apply a little something, it goes a long way," she said. Never mentioning why, she piled hers on a lot thicker than mine. So I asked about her habit of lining her eyes and lips with three different pencils.

"It's a Boriqua thing," Taking a long pause before answering. "It would look weird with your freckles and skin tone."

"Pasty and pencils don't mix?" We laughed.

During our months as roommates, near the heart of the nation's capital, Concepcion and I became inseparable. She was a neat freak, while I preferred to clean on the weekends. She had expensive taste in clothes, and despite our different sizes, she dressed me up every chance we were not in uniform. I traded in my Suave shampoo and conditioner for the "sulfate free" stuff that she promised would strengthen my hair even in a regulation sock-bun we wore on duty.

I picked up the phone and dialed her number again. Nothing. It was nearing five a.m. her time. What was I going to tell her? I had spoken to Blake in an internet café in Jordan. That meant he wasn't working for our government any longer. How much could we really help?

That was Concepcion, a better friend to everyone.

My reserved nature about new people made our friendship larger than life so far away from my family. She was comfortable around most people regardless of who they were and where they came from.

Concepcion was the rest of the world I always wanted to see. I was better for knowing her. I contemplated visiting her city a million times, but after a year of being away, I just wanted to go home. I wanted to taste my grandma's cherry cobbler with a side of homemade vanilla ice cream and finally buy a farm I had saved up for, a place to call my own. Iraq made me miss Missouri. The world would always wait for me, just like Concepcion would always be there. Only now, she wasn't.

I rolled out of bed and searched for the whiskey I kept in the house for family visits. Grandpa always played the fiddle better with a swig of Crown Royal. I shouldn't drink. I laced up my tennis shoes instead and ran into the dark alone.

We talked a lot while living an arm's distance apart about going into business together. One idea was to become a female bond enforcer, leather-clad mercenaries. I hated leather. Concepcion, on the other hand, started researching the business immediately, but once she realized she wasn't allowed to carry a firearm, her plans changed. She considered being an FBI agent. While in the Green Zone, she met a couple of agents at the Postal Exchange. She emailed back and forth with one. The agent was getting ready to retire and gave her some good contacts after she completed her tour.

Concepcion was not above using her feminine attributes to get the things she wanted, but every time I tried to play the woman card, I just felt wrong and uncomfortable.

It didn't help that I genuinely distrusted men in uniform, especially on deployment. They put females in two categories, bitch or slut. I chose to be more like the first one, way more fun. Somehow Concepcion had found a happy medium, and I went along for the ride. She was Ginger to my Mary Anne.

Though my mind kept replaying our friendship, somehow, I kept my body moving. I didn't have much time to pull myself together, but like so many other situations in life, I had to. I needed to do this.

Concepcion was a good person. I wanted the things for her that I guessed most women wanted: a family, a career, but mostly a longer life.

It was funny how I could plan what her life should have been like, but I had such a hard time living my own life. All the stereotypes about what a single woman is in these modern times were evaporating everywhere else except in Canton, Missouri, where being single and living alone was akin to having a terrible disease or dysfunction. My little sister was my only ally against my mom and two grandmas.

"Do you want to end up a crazy cat lady collecting Precious Moments figurines?" my mom asked. Did Precious Moments make one for two female soldiers? Would they understand our precious moments?

I would add that to my mom's Christmas list. What my mom really resented was that I wasn't getting any younger and I was still single.

I interviewed the first woman general who happened to be a state legislature. As a young private and budding military journalist, I wanted to know in the cheesiest way, "How do you do it?"

The general had ten minutes for an interview, but two hours later she was still explaining to me that making the rank of general wasn't a strategy or part of any plan. Her career happened because she had been in the right place at the right time. She happened to be what the government needed. She realized early on that only her experience meant she could be a general, and this was what she needed to do to make her time count. That was the key information I took away from the conversation, to play to my strengths.

Concepcion was jealous I was chosen for the interview. She wanted to ask her questions about her previous tours and make a connection for the future. I liked to pretend I was a real journalist instead of a mouthpiece for the chain of command.

During our training at Fort Meade, Maryland, we learned to tell the Army story. Not the truth. Concepcion made the news a pretty package with law and order prevailing. It was all I could do to find the oddities on the base and write up a four-page feature. I considered getting out of the life, but when Concepcion received her orders, I volunteered to go with the unit to Iraq. We retrained as military police officers. The plan was to beef up the MPs while the senior leadership of our unit toiled away in an air-conditioned office.

The training in Fort Leonard Wood was grueling. I realized there was a softer side of the military, and I had previously been in a less demanding role as a print journalist. Chapa excelled during the day with our long exercises in the punishing heat. She only ever got to see southern Missouri through a military lens, but an Army base was an army base. I had to wrap my knees with ice and bandages every night from banging them continuously during the stop, drop, and observe drills we practiced.

The one thing that gave me an assist was everyone

else on the squad underestimating my abilities. I repeated to myself during the training that I chose to do this, I chose to go with Chapa, and I was proud to serve with a good friend. She teased me about volunteering, but there was truth in what she said.

"Joelle, you volunteered because you don't know what else to do right now. It's an adventure away from life, and I'm your scapegoat. You just don't want to admit that you're a badass and you like this stuff."

One of my favorite things to train with was the paintball guns. It added a lightness to what we were doing. I remember entering a run-down building and watching two of my team members get hit with paintballs as they attempted to climb the stairs. I waited for the other team to come and check to see if everyone was down. I took out a team of four, one by one, as I hid the end of the staircase. Fish in a barrel if someone was patient enough. As I ascended the steps with my remaining team, we won the top prize of the day, which included a dinner out with the captain. Chapa was so mad her team lost, but I reminded her, smiling, "I was just being a badass, like you said."

Chapter Two

I walked into our local café, Grindhorse, on Main Street in Canton. The plan was to meet my nosy grandma for coffee and get some advice. My mind was still reeling from Concepcion's disappearance and the weight of Blake's request. It wasn't going well. Lack of sleep wasn't helping. Coffee should.

I spotted my dark, magenta-haired companion standing and chatting with the owner, a gray ceramic coffee mug in hand. She didn't see me as I smiled to Georgette, the owner slash head barista and current target of Grandma's curiosity. Georgette smiled back to me over Grandma's shoulder, who gestured back and forth as small amounts of coffee dripped onto the hardwood floor.

Oh, Grandma. The best storytellers always make a mess. At least she didn't slobber. Yet.

I picked up a napkin from a dispenser and quietly tiptoed beside her.

Georgette gestured to me. "Looks like you have company, Betty."

"She sure does."

Grandma Betty met my eyes and gave me a strong hug, scalding ceramic mug still in hand during our hug.

"It's Joelle. My hopeless soldier girl home to stay."

Why did she always say that? I'd been back a year.

"I was just telling Georgette here about the new pharmacist down at the drugstore."

"Really? Sounds like gossip to me."

Georgette nodded.

Grandma didn't take the bait. "He's single, of course, and he is just her type. He even knows how to cook."

"What's your type, Georgette?" I asked.

"Well, lately, just a pulse. I'm not picky, but not sure I should be taking on anything else besides this café."

Grandma nodded her head enthusiastically. She paused the nodding only to sip from her cup. "It's just so hard to find single men around here."

"And it seems like you're the local matchmaker, then. How's Grandpa?"

Grandma laughed and waved her free hand. "Oh, you know, Joelle, I meant for Georgette. It's been three years since her Lenny passed, and she has this whole business to take care of."

I considered her words. Why was I planning to ask this woman for advice? Simply because she was blood kin. The best thing that ever happened to Georgette was her husband dying of a heart attack at fifty years old. A known wife beater and philanderer, Lenny had kept Georgette docile and complicit for too many years.

This café was the smart bet Georgette took after she emerged with the life insurance money. Well earned and then some, she discovered she was a strong, savvy woman who could turn an empty storefront into a modern establishment in a small town near the Mississippi River. Yes, she was a beautiful woman, and her curse would be all the bored church ladies trying to bring her back into the marital fold, fresh from her success of regaining her independence. Georgette wasn't the only victim of well-intentioned meddling. I felt sorry for her only because my own grandma recently decided I needed a break from her declarations about my hardheaded ideas about happiness.

"You're going to wake up a spinster, Joelle, and

there is nothing you can do about it."

The words stung because when is the word *spinster* an affectionate term?

I examined Georgette's face. She looked away. It's funny how much we said without words.

"Why don't we let Georgette tend to her business and give her a break from romantic notions."

I was putting it mildly. Georgette visibly relaxed without sighing. Something I hadn't learned to avoid.

"May I get you some coffee, Joelle?"

"Yes, please. Cream and sugar." I handed her my debit card and a punch card with a chocolate-toned horse as a background. I was only two coffees away from a free fancier drink.

"Of course. Coming right up."

I looked around as Grandma escorted me to a two-top table facing the window that overlooked the street. Canton sure was coming back after two clean energy plants opened: one to make wind turbine blades and the other to process ethanol. I believed this was the future of the town. It was still up for debate in the mind of some old-timers. Everything was slower to change here.

"So, missy, what's on your mind?" Grandma got right to the point shortly after we settled into our seats.

"I've been adjusting to new management at the

newspaper. I appreciate you getting me in there."

Forget that I had a college degree from the best journalism school in the country. I was willing to work for ten dollars an hour, and I had to ask my grandma to put in a good word with the last publisher of the local *Canton Times*. Jobs in the arts never paid. Ever. She did, of course.

"The problem is Mr. Tom Montgomery handed everything over to his idiot daughter, who thinks we should get rid of the print version and just stick to Facebook," I said.

"Well, I don't know about that."

"Not sure she actually wants me to really write anything. She just wants her friends to write opinions about every local event."

My grandma finished the last of her cup. "That's no news. You look like the hair of the dog. What got you calling me at seven in the morning?"

"My friend Concepcion is sort of missing, and I can't believe no one's telling me anything."

"Yeah, you said something like that on the phone." This was the moment she savored before I had to ask for what I wanted.

My coffee came, and the moment was delayed longer.

A warm scone accompanied the coffee.

"Thanks, Georgette."

Georgette winked. She brought over the coffeepot and topped Grandma off.

"Well, what's the rush? She may be working on something for the FBI that we may not have information about."

"I thought about it, Grandma, I did. I was just wondering if you could inquire with your contacts in the political world to find out if she's okay."

Grandma took a deep breath. Her signature move. "I could do that. The question is, what happens if she is okay but unreachable?"

I sipped my coffee. I hadn't thought past knowing if she was okay. "I don't know. I guess I'm at that point where if she is on some mission and isn't helping on an immigration case, then I have to decide the next step for myself."

I took a bite of my scone. It was delicious and not because my stomach was roaring from hunger. It was. Georgette had the best scones I ever tasted. Scones weren't a Missouri thing. She brought us up in the world.

"You know I don't mind favors, Joelle. I just don't want to overplay my hand. I haven't decided if I'm going to donate again to a few campaigns. I don't like all this rhetoric about stand-your-ground laws. It just doesn't sound like common sense."

I cared less than she could imagine about her donations, but I nodded and took a few more bites. The truth was my grandma was a force of nature in this area of the state. At nineteen years old, she had finished college and worked as one of the first female coders for a radio manufacturer in the Midwest. Once, she told me about writing instructions for a machine that was the size of a house. After she left that role to start a family, the mathematical practice of her early twenties had led to her calculating soil fertilization on my grandpa's family farm. With her genius, the right seeds, and the right amount of water, Grandma became one of the most profitable farmers in the state. Forget doing the books. Grandpa had a scientist on his side.

Between the two of them, a real business grew, and Grandma was standing there right alongside a man with an elementary school education. She worked in her homegrown lab with her samples and later entered the tallest corn contest every year at the state fair and won for twenty-six years straight.

Eventually, the agriculture department of the US government had asked her to be a consultant for the Midwest, and she was. Politics entered the small town of Canton, and standing before me, meddling in the love lives of locals, was a calculating, experienced success.

That was why I was asking her for advice.

"I'll call around. It's not a big deal. I guess I should ask if you want to help the man you worked with. Concepcion may not be around to answer your questions."

"Now that I read Concepcion's letter about his story, I want you to help him. Just let me know if you can find her, Grandma."

I finished my scone as we sat in silence. I was glad to offload the burden of Hamdani's fate into the capable hands of a Washington insider.

Chapter Three

It was three long weeks before I heard anything from Grandma about Concepcion. She asked my little sister, LaLa, who worked as a St. Louis police officer, to be there and bring her work laptop. LaLa had previously worked on a task force, so her databases were linked to the military. It was all under the "working together" of modern law enforcement post-September 11th. We sat at her kitchen table as she detailed what she'd found out.

Grandma still had on makeup as she poured us glasses full of sweet tea. Her blue eyes shined through wrinkles formed around her face. I smiled and nodded.

She didn't smile back.

"I'm just going to come out and say that I can't say that anything about this is concrete."

LaLa was starting up her laptop. She was looking down at the keyboard while my grandma spoke. Had they spoken beforehand?

"Well, I didn't ask for facts. I just want to know where my friend is," I took a drink of tea. Why was there tension at my family table? Something was wrong.

"I don't want you to give up hope, Joelle, but I don't think your friend is coming back."

"Not coming back? Is she dead?"

"I don't know, and that's why this is so hard," she said. "I asked LaLa to consider a couple of things before we came back to you. It's hard to really say anything at this point."

I turned to LaLa. She breathed in and looked up at my grandma.

"We have a recent report of Concepcion Chapa dying in a car crash a month ago. She wasn't immediately identified because nothing about the car or the body led back to her identity. The body was badly burned."

"I don't understand. I heard nothing from anyone. Was there a funeral?" My eyes welled with tears, and I was crying.

"There wasn't a funeral; there wasn't an announcement. The only person who linked the body to her was Concepcion's immediate supervisor in the Miami office. She must have been on a case working undercover for her to be unidentifiable to everyone."

LaLa shook her head. This was hard for her, too. She had met Concepcion at my basic training graduation and always heard secondhand about our exploits together.

"This isn't even in the news. They aren't reporting it, and I was only able to find information because Grandma's got friends in higher places than the STL police." Her tone was defensive.

I looked at both of them. "When did you find out?"

Grandma put her hand on my shoulder. "Just today. I didn't tell you right away because there are too many unknowns here. I am not convinced Concepcion is really that Jane Doe."

"And neither am I, Joelle."

I took in a deep breath. Hope, even for a moment. "Just tell me what you know."

LaLa turned her laptop to show me the medical examiner's report. "Look at the date. It looks like it has Wite-Out on it. I shouldn't even have access to this. I think someone half-assed this document."

I looked at it. I could kind of see it, but I had the hint that the lettering was off.

"The date on this form is a week before I started asking questions," my grandma said. "I can't even tell you who I spoke to, but I didn't like the attitude of the young man who was on the phone with me. Everything was so 'inconvenient' while checking for it. That's not the way the government is supposed to work."

My heart pounded as I considered the back-and-forth. Was Concepcion missing, or was she dead?

"What else did you find?"

"Well, I spoke to the Miami office, and only a small group of people worked with her. In fact, just three. One of them was the supervisor who linked Concepcion to the Jane Doe."

I needed to lie down, but I kept drinking tea. The aura of diamonds in my eyes gave me an indicator one hell of a migraine was on its way. Of course.

"What should I do?"

"We don't know what's best. As your grandma, I must say that if my friend disappeared like this, I would keep searching, but something about this seems dangerous to me. I don't think anyone was counting on you checking. She was adopted as a teenager, right? Her adopted parents were refugees, are older, and haven't made any of this public. I'm not even sure who your friend really was."

"She was my fucking friend, Grandma. Who cares if she was adopted by refugees?"

My grandma shook her head and covered her face with her ringed hands.

"Grandma didn't mean it like that, Joelle, and you know it. What she meant was she called former and current senators working with the intelligence community about your friend, and she got a lot of blank stares. Then I found out more stuff that made this weird. Like how all the details are so vague. In my experience, most cases have a lot of unanswered questions. This just seems too clean to me. You don't get to blame this on us."

I examined her face, flushing with an intensity that made me quiet. "What do I do with this?"

"You need to stop asking that. You need to consider why your friend would disappear, on her own or with a case. You need to know that if she really died, then this would be a public matter. A single woman with a career in law enforcement and a military veteran would have been made a hero in the newspaper, yet nothing came. I don't think she is dead. I'd say to prove it to as many people as you can," LaLa stumbled through the last sentence.

My grandma shook her head and smacked LaLa on

the mouth. "The hell you will, Joelle. This is dangerous. Your friend is gone. I don't think dead, but she is not available. You should consider the fact that she wasn't opening up to you in the final months of her life, and I know this because I had her correspondence pulled and checked. Just wait. The truth always finds a way."

I had spoken to Chapa during the last few months, but one phone call didn't demonstrate what our friendship meant to me. It somehow became enough for me to think of her and say to myself, "I'll tell Chapa about that next time I speak to her." These things happened as we got older. I was less social and more introverted. The need to surround myself with strong personalities wasn't as important as when I was younger and deciding who to be, how to be. I wasn't volunteering anymore under the rules of friendship. I was sad about making less of an effort, but I wasn't alone in this. Chapa explained to me once that she rarely checked anything personal anymore. Neither of us were into social media at all. It united us further that we didn't blog about what we were having for breakfast, or weren't endlessly interrupted by pinging from our cell phones alerting us about someone's new Facebook photos.

Now I felt guilty about that. Maybe if we were texting every day, we would be more aware of what the other one was doing. Security was more important to her, though. She would never jeopardize her privacy or her job to be hip to what was new in the world. I didn't have my job as an excuse. In fact, I was pushed by the editor to put myself out there and develop a persona online to fuel traffic to *The Cantonian*'s social sites.

"I'll go pour my guts out online the moment you pay more for it," I said. That usually stopped the conversation. After the 2008 financial crisis, my excuses were wearing thin. Most small-town newspapers were going belly up or finally caving to publishing more ads than actual content.

At least Chapa could say her life depended on anonymity. What if someone found her somehow from her FBI work, and her death was real, maybe covered up, but real.

The silence was interrupted by my cell phone buzzing and ringing. I glanced at the caller ID, and it said Miami, Florida.

I flipped it open and mouthed, "Florida," to my sister.

"Hello?"

"Hello, is this Joelle McCoy?"

"It is."

"My name is Agnes Lopez, and I am a lawyer representing the estate of Concepcion Chapa…"

My head was pounding. The speaker was buzzing the hairs of my ears and drilling into my auditory channel. The voice kept going.

"Ms. Concepcion has passed away in a car accident."

"She did?"

"Yes, she did."

A few moments of silence ensued.

"Well, I was calling because…forgive me, you don't sound very surprised at your friend's death."

I swallowed. I was a terrible liar. "I just don't believe everything I hear, Ms. Lopez. Are you sure she's dead?"

Her voice went up an octave. "Of course I am. I have the details here from the county."

"Did you know her?"

"Yes, I did meet her once when we reviewed her will."

"Do you do a lot of wills for women in their twenties?"

Silence.

"It's a different world today. She was in a dangerous job."

I pulled the phone away from the verbal assault of Agnes Lopez's voice.

"Here's the thing. I don't believe it. I want you to

tell your client that I don't believe she's dead."

"I don't care if you believe it, Miss McCoy. I wouldn't waste my time with her estate if it wasn't true. When can you come down and receive the death benefit?"

"When you prove it to me."

I flipped the phone shut. My grandma and LaLa looked equally worried and proud at the same time. My small circle of friends just got even smaller.

It was seven a.m. when I pushed the blue button to call Blake Hamdani and give him the news. A beautiful sunrise got me out of bed with my bay window opened to the backdrop of a cornfield. I was preparing my first cup of coffee for the day when I missed his call from the kitchen. I tied my bathrobe a little tighter and washed my overnight creams off my face. I looked a little less scary on the webcam image.

"Hello…"

Blake's face appeared. Behind him was the backs of other people using the chain of computers in an internet café. I remembered doing the same on deployment. Such a cramped way to hear very personal conversations. Whole lives existed in all those phone calls.

"Hi, Blake," I waved like a five-year-old using Skype for the first time.

He smiled and waved back. He was skinnier in the face than I remembered. His eyes had bags worse than mine, and I had at least five years on him. Young people aren't supposed to look so old.

"Hi, McCoy. I'm glad you called back. I am very much glad that you called."

"I am glad to hear back from you. I am sorry, but I have some news that I wanted to share with you."

"Well, if it is sad news, let me go first. I have the best news. I heard from my caseworker for the immigration to your country, and she has told me Sergeant Chapa's paperwork will be enough. She will not have to be interviewed."

I feigned a smile and nodded. This was good news for him. I was happy she was still helping people, even with a letter.

"I am so glad about that. Let me know if I can help with anything else."

He nodded but held up his left hand. "Please, go ahead with your news. Your eyes are very sad today. I am sorry to see this."

Chapter Four

I focused on the colors whizzing by me as I sat behind the wheel of my sister's Kia Sorento. The green of Kentucky seemed richer somehow against the gray cement of the road. I needed to stretch my legs in the worst way, but I shouldn't complain. LaLa was officially on break from driving after she declared her cruise-controlled seven hours enough for one day, and her legs were as long and cramped as mine. I didn't want us to stop longer than a few minutes.

Oddly, I was driven to drive to my best friend's funeral above all other things. She wasn't really dead, I told myself, but I still had doubts. Did the fact that her lawyer had hastily planned a church service with her adopted parents create more or less doubt in the veracity of this story? I couldn't tell. I would always show up for her, though, even in spirit.

I passed a road sign that signaled another hour to our next planned stop.

"Hey, what are you thinking about?" I turned down the speaker on NPR moderating a deep discussion on tomato plant care.

"Just work stuff," she said. "It's been crazy with Axel and my shifts. It's always opposite, and I spend more time without him than with him."

"That sounds good to me." I laughed until she punched my arm in retribution.

"That's not fair. I know he's not your favorite, but he's police, he's hot, and he gets me."

I rubbed my arm with my free hand. She punched hard, and I would probably have a bruise. "Yeah, he's something. What bothers me is he isn't at your level intellectually. It's like he's missing a neuron or two. He doesn't make the connection to any of our political discussions and doesn't seem to care to know."

"Well, it's not like everyone cares about that stuff like us. It can be nice not to have to argue my point with him on anything. He just concedes."

"I just think more of you. We're in public service

for a reason. He's the guy that checks out all of our racks and says stuff like 'Guns are cool. I like guns.' He thinks he's being funny, but you have to be smart to actually be funny."

"Not true. A lot of comedians are dumb."

"Not the good ones."

We sat in silence for several minutes. My mind wandered against the backdrop of LaLa punching out a message on her phone. My feelings about the funeral were just below my surface of calm. I had cried unsatisfying tears prior to the trip when I had received the hurried phone call from Ms. Lopez. Somehow the woman had managed to call it a celebration of life ten times in the span of a short conversation.

If anything, calling it a celebration of life was like an affirmation that Concepcion Chapa was alive and still deciding the fate of her last party. I relented my stance about not going when my grandma threatened to slap me silly over the phone.

"It's your duty," Grandma said. "Put yourself in her situation, and you'll decide what is right."

Uh, friends not dying is the right thing. I would go to any party to celebrate it.

A Black Lexus keeping in line with an RV blocked me from passing.

"Oh fuck."

LaLa looked up from her screen and watched the two vehicles ahead. She laughed.

"What's so funny?"

She pointed through the windshield, "Look at the spare tire on that RV. It says 'we sleep around.' That's smart and funny."

We both laughed. "And it says they're from Missouri. Of course, they're from our great state. 'I'm from Missouri; you have to show me,'" I said, in my best hillbilly drawl.

The conversation lightened, and by the time we reached the hotel in Miami the next day, all arguments were over.

"Is her family going to be there?" LaLa asked. "I mean her adopted family."

"They will be there, according to the lawyer. I haven't met most of her other friends. The only people I will know are other soldiers. She should have some colleagues from the FBI, too. It makes me sad I never visited like I said I would. We talked about these grand plans of working together down here."

"That's not fair, Joelle. It works both ways, and she didn't visit, either."

We arrived at the funeral late after we got stuck trying to find a parking spot. The church next to the funeral home was packed to capacity. It looked like a going-away ceremony with all the uniforms, military and police, gathered in one place. I opted to wear a black silk dress covered in Stargazer lily patterns all over the bottom.

I was dressed for a wedding, not for a funeral. As beautiful as all of the flowers and people dressed in their finest were, it seemed carefully curated near the front.

"This wasn't what I was expecting," I whispered to LaLa.

She accepted a coffee from an attendant near the sign-in book. It smelled strong and dark.

"What did you expect? Her to jump out and yell 'Boo' at you? Let's hold all opinions for later. I want to check out some of these hotties in here."

"Shameless." I nodded. "They probably all think Concepcion loved them best, but I know the truth. She loved me best."

"Now who's bullshitting? This is an odd group for a funeral. I can't spot any true civilians."

We found room in the fourth row out of fifteen. It was pew seating, and I shoved in next to an older black man. He smelled like aftershave and discipline in his dress blues. He handed me a one-page bulletin of the events. It listed out the next half hour as though we had to thoroughly account for our time.

"How did you know Concepcion?" I asked.

He didn't turn his large torso to me but kept staring at the seat in front of him. "She was my recruit."

I breathed in. This was hard. The loss had seemed so much smaller in Canton, Missouri. It was really real here.

"Thank you for recruiting her, Sergeant. I served with her."

"Good to hear. It's a damn shame."

"Yes, it is," LaLa handed me a pack of travel Kleenex. I waved her off. Not yet. Not ready.

The service started with Agnes Lopez, her lawyer, thanking everyone for attending. The sadness of a paid employee being her representative was not lost on me. She was still bankrolling her own existence. It was cleaner this way. I wasn't ready to answer any questions about this to anyone.

A simple prayer from a perfectly acceptable version of a religious man. He had the beard and all. Not sure what denomination, but it didn't matter. I looked around and saw people of all ages and colors equally in bewilderment and stages of grief. I saw an older Southeast Asian couple with eyes cast down to the wood floor.

I nudged LaLa. "That's got to be her parents for sure."

"Do you think that hot guy over there is a cousin or something? He's definitely delicious."

"I'm the wrong one to ask. He could be in the military or something. He's got a bulge on the right side."

"Good eyes."

The pastor started again after the organ player finished with a three-minute version of "Amazing Grace." The pastor came up. He resembled Chong from Cheech and Chong. He was the spitting image.

"Concepcion Chapa lived and died as a hero in her own way. Her tremendous sacrifice brings the best of you here today to celebrate her life. We cannot know what reasons our creator had for taking such a young, vibrant woman from our lives so early, but we can take this time to reflect on a life well lived. Discipline and dedication define the legacy of Concepcion Chapa, who, at a young age, had her own parents taken from her too soon. Parents who loved their own child so much that they entrusted her upbringing to the two best people they had ever met in their lives, Jimm and Chantrea Mao. As each one of you reflect on your memories with Concepcion, please think about how you can be a light for her legacy in the world. And now we will finish today's ceremony with a prayer and open the doors to our adjoining room for refreshments and good music."

I closed my eyes while he prayed. My feet and legs tingled with the numbness of perpetually sitting. This wasn't what I imagined. I couldn't cry. It wasn't real. Her loss was temporary. I was sure of it.

"Remember out of the darkness comes the light."

With that phrase ringing in my ears, I opened my eyes. I looked over at LaLa. She still had her hands held together. She was looking intently at something in the distance. Focused.

"LaLa, did you hear that?"

"Hear what?"

"Out of the darkness comes the light," I whispered, staring forward.

"I didn't hear that."

"What? He just said it."

I looked over at the sergeant. He was crying. I couldn't ask.

Later, after most of the people filed over to the cake and coffee in the room next door, I pushed my way past a few shorter Hispanic women to reach the pastor.

He waved me over when I met his eye. "Who do I have the pleasure of meeting today, young lady?"

"I'm one of her friends—well, she was my best friend," I was ashamed of my hesitation in claiming this distinction.

"Sure, I understand. Did you resonate with the service today, Joelle?"

I hadn't said my name, so I looked down to see if I was wearing a name tag. He noticed me noticing.

"I know who you are. I had the benefit of looking at her apartment and her home. There were several photos of you in many of her memory books."

"Yes, we spent a lot of our twenties together in random places. Listen, the reason I wanted to speak with you is about what you said at the end. Out of the darkness comes the light."

His eyes searched mine. "Excuse me."

"Out of the darkness comes the light," I repeated.

"I'm sorry, you must have misheard. I didn't say that exactly. I repeated a Bible verse I found outlined in one of the old Bibles on her shelf. It was dated a few years ago by a chaplain from your deployment. Let me say it again." He closed his eyes. "I saw that wisdom is better than folly, just as light is better than darkness." Ecclesiastes 2:13.

I swallowed hard. "Light is better than darkness. Damn, that's some deep stuff to underline, Chapa."

He smiled. "On the contrary, it is very simple. I hope we helped to bring you a sense of peace in all of this, Joelle."

I nodded. It was a lying nod. "*We?*"

"We as in her family and Ms. Lopez, of course. You were a very good friend to her, from what I saw. What did she mean to you, Joelle?"

I didn't answer. I was sure this man wasn't a pastor and was pumping me for information. Paranoia was a bitch.

"It's funny you picked that phrase about light and darkness, because she was the most real person I have ever met. Street smart, self-aware, and she called out my naivety. She was better than me at life, period. I can only see that now that she's gone." I stared past the pastor, searching for LaLa. "Time and distance apart left a big hole in my life. One that I don't think can ever be filled. But I guess I'll have to try, right."

"Right,"

"Thanks, pastor," I said as I found LaLa in the crowd. My face flushed, and I placed my hand on my neck. My pale skin was burning up.

I met her eyes and mouthed the words, "Let's go."

"Why do we have to go? We haven't even met her parents or her work friends."

I snapped my head and met her eyes. "Don't tell me you're trying to hit on a bunch of dudes in Florida at my best friend's funeral."

"Fuck you, Joelle. I wasn't trying to do that. I just thought it would help you to meet people who loved her like you did."

"None of these people know what our friendship was like. I'm not a good version of myself right now. I am freaking the fuck out about this pastor. I don't think he's legit."

I pulled her arm as we weaved through the crowd of people stirring powdered creamer into Styrofoam cups. They didn't even spring for the good stuff. I hated that powdered shit.

"Okay, yeah. Once you start freaking out on the clergy, it's time to roll. Can we at least stop somewhere before we leave?"

"Like where?" I gestured toward the car.

"Like at the beach, to see the ocean really quick."

"Yes, we can." I smiled. "Thanks for coming here with me, LaLa." And I meant every word. The beach was one place Concepcion Chapa said she remembered being at a lot with her birth parents before they died. It was her place. Her thing. I just wasn't going to get to see it with her.

My eyes filled with tears.

Chapter Five

I was working when Concepcion's lawyer found me again. I was putting the finishing touches on the county-fair issue for the community newspaper I worked at, and the phone at my desk just kept ringing. I picked it up on the fourth ring after I recognized a Miami area code, Concepcion's area code.

"Hello, Joelle McCoy speaking."

"Miss McCoy, this is Agnes Lopez. I'm glad I was finally able to get a hold of you," A fakeness dripped from her voice. "I'm calling on behalf of Concepcion Chapa's estate."

"Ma'am, I'm sorry, but I'm on a deadline here. Is there any way I can call you back later? Unless you have some proof you want to talk to me about," Who was I kidding? This was not the news desk at the *New York Times*. I was working on formatting livestock auctions and the advertising for a former *American Idol* contestant who was coming to the Missouri State Fair.

The woman on the other end of the phone line took a deep breath. I paused. I was a little too firm in my refusal.

"No, I do not, and we cannot speak later. I have been trying to get in touch with you for six months, and I cannot put off closing the will any longer," she sounded pissed off.

My mind glazed over her request. Six months, had it been six months? What she doesn't get is I don't believe Chapa is dead. Not then and not now.

"I need to know what to do with your share of the estate. I have an account with four hundred thousand dollars with your name on it. I don't care what you do with it, but I need these papers signed this week. If another week passes, then her parents do not get the money she allotted for them. She specified you both go together. She wanted you there for her family. All we need for proof here is the death certificate."

"Please, ma'am. Just tell me what I need to do," I answered.

"Well, I could fax this to you, but…" She paused.

"No buts. But what?" I said. "Us military girls just need to hear the facts. I could sue you for proof of her death."

"Sue me for proof of my client's death? Well, the state can just take the money, then. Concepcion was like you, too. I wanted to let you know her parents prepared some of her items from your deployment together. I think you meeting with them would be best. Maybe they can provide answers. They both were saddened that you didn't meet them at the funeral."

"Oh, I guess I didn't realize they wanted to meet me. That funeral was weird, so all I wanted to do was get outta there."

"I also faxed your office a copy of a letter to the State Department for the Hamdani visa. It is authenticated by a document's expert, so her passing really shouldn't hinder her statement."

After I hung up, I pulled the fax from the machine. It was only the letter, not the estate papers. I read it again. It was the same letter Blake had sent over in our first Skype call.

"My name is Concepcion Chapa, former sergeant in the United States Army, Public Affairs Unit. I work for the government in the Miami office of the FBI. I am a proud American who served my country alongside Blake Hamdani in different parts of Iraq. I am writing

on his behalf to explain what a true-blue ethical human being he is. His father was a translator beginning just after the invasion in 2003. You can review his file under 'Justice' Hamdani. His mother worked as a radio host for the US forces to support our integration efforts. His father was gunned down on his way home from work at the base. It was one of the earliest killings of a translator, and, sadly, it discouraged many from serving with us.

"His mother, Rashida, continued working with us despite the danger and took on extra laundry duties to supplement her income. By Iraqi standards, they lived a middle-class life prior to the death of Blake's father. Blake continued to study and earned his engineering degree in Jordan prior to his father's death. After his death, he returned to help his mother and started working the exact position that killed his father. I met Blake in 2007 when he worked with our unit. He integrated with the soldiers and treated us to local homecooked food whenever his mom cooked something special.

"One afternoon, he came dangerously close to losing his life when a Humvee rolled over an IED. I was sure he was going to quit after it happened. He was educated and the best translator we had when interrogating other Iraqis. I have never written a letter

like this, and I do so now because we need people like Hamdani to keep fighting alongside us. The dream of our values must be real. As we scaled down the war, translators like Hamdani lost their jobs and couldn't find work because of the reputations of working with us. It's time we stand up for the Hamdanis and allow a capable engineer to pursue his dream of working with us once again. I have put Blake in touch with several NGOs that can help support him and his mother once arriving here.

"Please expedite his case and grant him the same courtesy he gave us after he came to work on our behalf. If you won't do it for him, do it for me. As a female veteran who continues to work for her country, I plead for his safety. He sacrificed more in the years I worked with him than many people will in a lifetime."

I was proud of her for writing the letter. It brought me back to the reason I was still holding out hope for her. I researched suspicious deaths and found plenty of conspiracy porn to keep me clicking away on sites that, as a journalist, I could clearly see were based on innuendo and scraps of information. I wasn't taking my family's words of caution seriously because I wanted to believe that Chapa was an exception.

Why did she give me money? I couldn't shake the last conversation about me wanting to lead a different life. A life of travel that needed more money. It was only talk. I wanted to impress my friend somehow so she wouldn't give up on me. She always had something exciting going on with her team. The only case she told me about involved black-market goods from war-torn countries being sold in the wealthier circles of Palm Beach—antiquities. It all had to do with tax evasion in the end. I couldn't follow all of the details, but I listened with envy at how the saga continued with Chapa at the helm.

After my grandma and LaLa came up with little more than they originally found, I became more withdrawn in the vague mysteries that seemed choreographed in detail about government conspiracy posts. The funeral hadn't helped anything, but I checked out the pastor and reviewed his church's website. He was an active participant with photos to prove he was a legitimate pastor. It didn't mean he wasn't a part of something or retired from something else. My imagination and gut feelings were leaving me more confused with everything I found out.

I learned more than I cared to about all of the corruption in Washington circles and anonymous sources who felt compelled to blow the whistle. One of the blogs demonstrated a close case to Chapa's disappearance but involved a super-sketchy guy who supposedly worked for the National Security Agency. This tale was told from his ex-wife's point of view, who was clearly upset about a measly two-hundred-thousand-dollar death benefit owed to their children. She was convinced it was all a setup so he could avoid, number one, being a father and, number two, paying the private school tuition of their two children.

I sent the link to my sister, and she immediately revealed the holes in the woman's story and the inconsistencies involved. She did look up the guy's case and said the body was never found, and he was believed to have died under suspicious circumstances.

It was enough to convince me to hold out hope for my own conspiracy theory, but I wasn't brave enough to post about it. I wasn't quite ready to examine the holes in her death. Instead, I decided the visit to Chapa's parents could hopefully provide a salve to missing my friend.

Chapter Six

I wished I was there for any reason other than sitting in the waiting room of the Veterans Affairs hospital, going in for a therapy session. It was part of my monthly sessions to move forward and find out what I wanted to do with my life, especially my career. I stopped checking the internet for answers and booked my plane ticket to visit Miami again, this time under better circumstances. I tried so much not to think of my friend and her fate that I didn't really have time to do anything else.

After the funeral, my therapist diagnosed me with complicated grief disorder, or CG, as she so patiently explained. It was common for people like me—veterans with a history of mental stress and anxiety, not to mention alcohol abuse. But the way the woman said it so matter-of-factly, it made me smile and nod while at the same time deciding it was over between me and her. All of the things she listed were so common that I could have had everything and nothing wrong with me. I wasn't interested in her pills or her pushy attitude because even if I had something like CG, I didn't want to forget Chapa. This was why I needed to make this trip despite how nervous I was about facing her parents.

A few months later, I was paired up with the latest member of the St. Louis mental health team, a young woman who had served in the Air Force. I was hopeful of making progress. There were bags under my eyes, and I was feeling tired lately, so I hoped she could help me sleep.

"What do you want to talk about today, Joelle?" Dr. Jodi Pepper asked. My mouth curled into a smile every time I saw her name. I just couldn't get over it.

I sat in a chair in the medical exam room—no couches for us vets. With cost-cutting, many of the professionals were all housed in the ancient VA hospital versus private offices with all the perks of a cushy chair. It didn't matter in the end, as I was accustomed to a no-frills health care experience.

"I keep thinking about how I could have done something different. Last night, I dreamt that I forgot to tell her I still have her Turkish belly dancing belt we bought in a market together. The previous night, I wanted to tell her about an old man I saw in the grocery store who bought a bunch of candles. Really trivial stuff. Who cares if I have the wrong balaclava and it says Chapa inside mine. I don't even use it."

"Were those things important to her?" The doctor opened her notebook before looking down and transcribing everything I said, word for word. She barely made eye contact. The fact she appeared to be listening to me was an improvement.

I shook my head. "No, it wasn't. We were always sharing things and switching things. I don't know how many years I have had the balaclava and noticed it was hers but forgot to tell her. Now it's a thought that keeps me up for three hours."

We discussed my medication and if my mind was racing or my heart pounding. I hated this part. It gave me a victimhood feeling. I wasn't a victim of anyone but my own mind.

I talked, and she listened.

"I noticed you stated she was better than you as a soldier. Do you really feel she was better than you at your job?"

I thought about her question. I didn't realize I'd even said that aloud. *Better* was a strong word. She was good. She was the best. What was I in comparison?

"We both had things we were good at. She seemed to get along better with all the guys. I wasn't used to being ignored as much as I was in the military. It wasn't like school, where a teacher forced it to be more equal in the classroom. I just did what I was told. Sometimes that made me the best, and sometimes it made me like every other asshole trying to prove herself."

My voice sounded alien to me. Whiny and emotional. No wonder I was ignored. And, yes, I was ignored by men when Concepcion was around. But I never realized how much it had bothered me until now.

"Give me an example where you excelled over your friend or your team. What is something you walked away with after your training experience?"

I took a drink from my glass water bottle. I ran my hands through my hair and looked down at my lap. I couldn't think of anything.

"I can't think of anything. My time in Iraq was so fucked up. I just wanted to be out of there most of the time. She wanted to be there."

I stared at my slip-on ballet flats. They had zero arch support, and they made my back hurt, but I could be careless in the civilian world.

"Was there another time? Maybe when you weren't on the deployment where you felt like you were fully engaged and proud of yourself? I'm trying to find a way for you to connect to your own experience in a different way than including your friend. You are always summing up things and rarely reflecting on the details of those experiences. What shaped *you*?"

I saw the doctor's face flush in intensity, and for a moment, she met my eyes with her request. *Bravo, doctor. You're trying to understand me here.*

I thought of graduating basic training and how proud I was, but all those memories included her graduating, too. There was a basic standard set, and we both met it. We were successful together.

"I'm still thinking of things that include her, Doctor."

She nodded in understanding. "That's okay. It's normal for our friends to take on a larger-than-life role after these big moments of our experience. The Army forged that bond and that friendship for a purpose, and it really, really works. I have men in here still talking about their Concepcion Chapas from forty to sixty years ago. It doesn't end. What I want to find is something you are proud of about you, regardless of if she was there."

I laughed shyly at her insistence. This woman was

probably five years older than me, and she seemed to get to the heart of my problem. So much for the VA sucking at everything.

I fixed my gaze to the edge of the paper covering the long table.

"This one time in training, I survived the only unplanned attack during our simulation training. I guess that was kind of cool. My dad loves when I tell that story."

She met my eyes. "Tell me that one. I get paid to hear your stories."

I set the scene of our final mission of basic training before we could graduate, which included a ten-mile ruck march in the South Carolina heat that lasted through the night after camping for four days in the wilderness. Fire ants, bug spray, and camouflage, with baby-wipe showers for the private parts.

"Chapa and I got in trouble from our drill sergeant for crossing our eyes at each other when he was talking." The resulting punishment took weeks to unfold, and we realized it right before our bivouac on the final mission.

"We were assigned to carry the squad automatic weapon, called the SAW, for third platoon while the rest of the guys carried M16s. That meant twenty-two pounds with blank ammo carried in my arms while the rest of the people had eight pounds on the front. Everyone had forty pounds on their backs. It was not an ideal scenario for someone whose nickname *Chicken Wing* was written in chalk on my Kevlar for safety reasons."

She listened and wrote notes. I noticed a smile when I recounted my nickname for my long scrawny arms. "Monkey arms," my sister called them.

I told the doctor about the march to the campsite and how I had to dig a foxhole with the only other tall girl in the squad, who we called the Jolly Green Giant.

"When night fell, they separated us all to stand guard in our foxholes. The Jolly Green Giant fell right asleep as we stood up facing the trees. I was tired and realized I could prop myself up using the stand of the SAW and rest my forehead. I almost fell asleep. It wasn't the first time on guard duty that I thought I would pass out from exhaustion.

"About two in the morning, I heard the trees rustling in front of me. I waited for a few moments and realized someone was walking straight into my watch zone. I was scared and poked the girl next to me, but she was snoring.

"So I did what our drill sergeants said and yelled the challenge question, 'Where's the eagle?' I waited for the password to come back as the word *yellow*. It was nonsense, but that was the point. Everyone memorized the question and the passwords so we could walk safely around the camp."

The doctor leaned forward. "What happened?"

"I didn't hear the word, so I yelled two more times. Despite the silence, I kept hearing the walking and saw the trees shaking. I finally said, 'If you don't tell me the password now, I am going to let this thing go.'"

"The SAW?"

"Yes, the SAW. I had only fired a SAW once, but it fires automatically if you hold the trigger, so I basically fired like thirty blanks into the trees, and I heard someone running away. It was so crazy. All the other soldiers around us woke up to the noise. The adrenaline was pumping through me, and my weapon got hot with all the blanks going through it. I remember how scared I was."

"Was it another soldier messing with you guys?"

I crossed my legs and shook my head. "No. It wasn't. My drill sergeant came running over right after and yelled for me to get out of the foxhole and report to his station. He looked angry, but then he smiled. He was such an asshole ninety percent of the time, but he said, 'McCoy, you just fired at the captain, the captain who forgot the password and who is so proud of you now that he is challenging people all over the camp. He wants to see if his troops are prepared. He has never been fired at with a shitload of blanks before.'"

"Oh my gosh. That is such a good story. Your dad was right to make you tell it again."

I smiled. "The only bad thing was Concepcion did fall asleep on her SAW, and the captain caught her after me, so the next day she was low crawling on the gravel for messing up."

She nodded. That was the moment she stopped understanding the military life. It was all fun and games. When we were tested, someone was a winner, and someone was a loser.

She checked her watch and set us another appointment. Maybe I was getting somewhere.

When I left, she handed me a prescription for sleeping pills. The secret password must have been yellow.

Chapter Seven

Cramped. I struggled to make the most out of my tiny seat on the airplane on my way to Miami. It didn't help that my neighboring passenger had to have a seatbelt extender and was overflowing in my small space.

A sharp pain in my left knee jolted me back into my seat as the flight attendant pushed the drink cart up the aisle. Damn, she hit my kneecap. I extended my legs as much as I could, which meant they were smashed against the back of the seat with a businessman working away on his laptop.

"Fuck," the starched, stiff man uttered a curse word intended for me. I always forgot this rigmarole until I was on another airplane, flying somewhere else, when

I would realize I was not the ideal height to fly on the smaller jets.

Give me a bucket seat on a C-130. At least my legs could extend as far as the large black box filled with green duffel bags. Though a military aircraft came with a certain sense of anxiety, I could somehow sleep the entire way. Someday I would be able to afford first class, but not when airlines were nickel and diming me every step of the way.

I closed my eyes. Concepcion and I had flown together both military and commercial. We were once upgraded to first class while on leave because we were in uniform. Concepcion saved everything they gave us. Two grown women stuffing the freebies in our regulation "purses" made from the carrying bags for claymore mines. The commander was happy to explain to his superiors why we had drab green bags while on missions, but instead of an exploding weapon, we had tampons, gum, and baby wipes galore. Others less concerned with vanity would carry those items in the proper cargo pockets built in the uniform.

The "huge tumor growing out of the sides of our legs" look was not for me. I mean, what female wants to make her thighs look bigger, especially in uniform? I glanced down at my own shiny leather purse and enjoyed being a civilian. I hoped the leather look was in style.

My hosts for this trip, Jimm and Chantrea, were waiting dutifully for me at the gate, with a large sign. I couldn't miss them. It helped that I had seen them at the funeral, but the coward in me had left before I had a chance to meet them.

"Welcome to Miami, Joelle," Jimm set down the poster board with my name written in huge letters, elegant strokes from an elegant couple. I'd never had a sign for an airport pickup. It was a sweet touch.

Jimm took my bags while Chantrea searched her purse for something. She retrieved a small baggie.

"Here is some sticky rice and beef jerky," she handed me a foil packet, perfectly wrapped with care. "Sticky rice is perfect to take to go. It's Asian fast food for you today, Miss McCoy."

"Thank you," I meant it. "I haven't had sticky rice before, but it looks like food, so I'm in."

I was starving and hadn't felt like buying peanuts to eat in such cramped quarters.

"You can eat while Jimm gets the car. There is a lot of traffic, so it takes a while until we are home."

I graciously accepted the snack, listening as Chantrea updated me on what she and her husband had planned for me. We could go shopping and visit the beach whenever I wanted. Then she paused and furrowed her brow as if she had to remember how to say her next sentence.

"Ms. Lopez, the lawyer, needs to talk to us first before we get busy with our other plans."

I nodded. At times, I forgot my friend was gone. Chantrea seemed cautious about the meeting but happy about my visit.

I planned to stay a week so the business of why I was there wouldn't seem rushed or impersonal.

"Don't worry about me, LaLa," I had said when she dropped me off at the airport in St. Louis. "It's time I face the music alone."

I had to see Concepcion's city myself. I wasn't focused on the details of her death the last time I was here. The shock was wearing off, and I wanted to know who else was involved in the accident. I wanted to know what she had been doing since I had seen her. I wanted to be a comfort to her parents and not be remembered by them as cold and indifferent like I appeared at the funeral. Despite my efforts, I still had no idea how to change my attitude toward all of this.

I finished my homemade snack and feigned a smile to Chantrea just as Jimm rounded the corner in his immaculately clean Lexus SUV.

"I am glad I'm here," I said, hoping she could read my feelings, my sincerity.

"We're going to make this fun," she smiled. "I don't get too many visitors. You know, you need to see what Miami has to offer." She motioned with her tiny manicured hand covered in various-sized diamonds and gold jewelry.

"Yes, I do."

Once in the suburbs of Miami, I settled into the guest bedroom. I unpacked a few of my essentials and climbed into the spacious shower to wash the flight off my skin. I smelled lavender in the bathroom and noticed the exact brand of shampoo and conditioner that Concepcion used sitting on the inside shelves. I blinked through the tears, remembering our Cher-in-the-shower moments, and let the water wash away the pain on my face. I slowly relaxed and let myself softly cry for my friend. I was here, and this was the right moment to face everything.

What would living in Miami be like? The temperature alone would keep me barely clothed year-round, and that sounded a little sexier to me than bulging winter coats and dry skin.

I had a week to try on a new city, even if my plans

were not all peaches and cream. Who knows? Maybe I would discover something here unexpected.

The water trickled down on me, and the steam rose on the travertine walls.

The money was a distraction. I pictured the bank account balance. Four hundred thousand dollars in checking—no, wait, savings. That was right, savings. Concepcion's death benefited me? I started to tear up. The damage was done. I missed my friend.

As we sat in the formal dining room, I noticed Chantrea was not eating much. With a table full of my favorite curries and rice noodle mixtures, I couldn't understand why.

"Everything is so delicious," My eyebrows raised. "Chantrea, why aren't you eating?"

The fifty-something-year-old petite woman smiled, happy I had noticed her willpower. "I'm on a new diet," she explained, "no eating after seven."

"Sure, Chantrea," Jimm glanced at me and the food in front of us.

He ate while looking at his own plate. The quiet man seemed to be cracking the slightest of smiles. I searched Chantrea's face for answers.

"Don't listen to him," Chantrea said. "He eats

everything and never gains anything. I eat a little and gain weight everywhere."

"You eat while you cook," Jimm said. "You eat your half while I wait it out in the living room."

"I have to taste it; otherwise you complain there's not enough spice. It's your fault."

I smiled. I wanted to be married long enough to have someone else know me and call me out on my bullshit. Jimm did that for Chantrea.

Concepcion said her adoptive parents had a similar dynamic to her real parents. Though from very different cultures, cooking, eating, and family were a big part of their lives. I thought about the next day's events, where I would go and visit Concepcion's biological relatives. The ones unfit to care for her. It would give me a greater insight into where she came from. If anything, they deserved a visit from a friend.

"You act like she was a fucking saint or something," the woman practically spitting on me while she spoke. I wasn't one hundred percent sure if she had false teeth or a lisp. It didn't matter, saliva was still flying. Why did I come here, why? I should have listened to Chantrea when she warned me against visiting Concepcion's aunt, Ana.

"You aren't family, *chica*," Ana shook her head, as if I didn't know we were not related.

"Ma'am," I started to interrupt. I couldn't silence my heart pounding from so much adrenaline.

"Don't start that 'ma'am' shit with me. I loved my niece more than you ever could. Before she joined the military, she wanted to be there for us. She was going to stay here and take care of us. It doesn't surprise me she died like she did; it's dangerous out there, and she was looking for a fight. I think there's something more to it."

I started to ask what but stopped myself mid-sentence. Did I want to know what she thought about my suspicions into Chapa's death? I doubted Ana would begin to understand why I was convinced she wasn't dead. I wondered what would happen if I gave this lady some of Chapa's benefit. She probably wouldn't use it for anything good, but then that was me judging people again.

"Listen, we don't want to hear about money anymore. We are doing fine just like we are," she continued. "Once the lawyer told us she gave the money to you, she was dead to me. I mean, you haven't got any kids, and you have your whole life to make more. I'm almost forty years old."

She was at least fifty-five. Or had she led a hard

life of drug addiction? No amount of Miami sun did that much damage. The rouge and harlot-colored lipstick didn't help matters.

"At least she didn't give it all to those Asians. They raised her for three years, and now they deserve a check. That don't sit right with me. We were blood."

Concepcion had barely mentioned them, so there had to be a reason why she chose not to leave them anything. It was obvious where it would go, right into the veins of an addict.

The tiny two-bedroom apartment smelled like mothballs. I wanted to gag.

"Let me tell you something," she stepped up to me, the top of her head meeting my chin, just like Concepcion. Her expression changed, and I noticed her humanity. "If you started giving out money, then everyone's gonna want something. We got a big family. Concepcion had the smarts to go somewhere and do something. I know how hard she had it; a hell of a lot harder than your corn-picking bony ass…"

Her eyes welled with tears. She cursed the saints and lit a Virginia Slim. Oh, the irony. There was nothing slim about her.

I started to see something like pride for her niece. She must have been happy when her niece made it out of here. Now, she was gone, just like her parents.

"Concepcion got pregnant at going on fourteen years old. I bet you didn't know that," Ana said.

I did know.

"She had an abortion, and my sister about killed me because I had the brains enough to take her to get it. She didn't want to listen to nobody, but she was a little like me at that age."

The aunt retold many of the negative experiences Concepcion had confided to me. I didn't stop the lady. It had been a long year and a half in Iraq. Concepcion and I had talked about everything under the sun that happened in our short lives, just to talk and not hear the outside noises.

During night shifts on guard duty, I learned that Concepcion felt a lot of guilt about what she had put her parents through. It was those nights, looking up at the stars and spilling our secrets, that it was more like I was in high school again at a slumber party back home. No matter how I might have judged her then, with my own mundane past, now was not the time to cast any stones. I knew I couldn't stop this woman from spewing out Concepcion's misgivings.

"So, when her parents died, why didn't you or the rest of the family raise her?"

"We couldn't have handled her like they did. They had more of everything than us. They offered, and I wasn't going to deny my niece a better life," Ana said.

Now who was acting like a heroine?

"But she's family," I wanted to make her sweat, feel guilty for badmouthing the dead.

"Weren't you listening? She already had one abortion, and you didn't see the way she looked at my Ricardo," Ana was coming back to her two-faced self. "She would have had two before she was legal. She always liked my boyfriends. I bet she had a lot of buddies in the Army, right?" She snickered and ashed her third cigarette.

"You're right, your slut of a niece told me to forget her whore of an aunt when I made my rounds with her life insurance money," I shouted. "Something about 'it takes one to know one.'"

I was already standing when I started my tirade. I left out of her screen door into the hot, Miami sun. I was exhausted from the topic of Concepcion's past, but happy I could leave knowing I opened every door.

Chapter Eight

"Miss Joelle, you should stay another week," Chantrea was helping me fold the laundry, which was supposed to go into my open suitcase.

"I need to get back," halfheartedly preparing my excuse. "The newspaper will be waiting. We have a small staff."

"You need a vacation. They'll understand. When do you *ever* go on vacation? You are like Concepcion, all work and no play. You haven't even met her friends. Well, her other friends. Nice men. They come visit us when they can."

"Like from high school or the neighborhood?" I

asked.

"Oh, no, her friends from work. I think she was dating one of them."

I recalled Concepcion mentioning a boyfriend, but I didn't think it was serious. She usually changed the subject quickly once she realized I wasn't particularly excited about anything resembling the military. She must have heard in my voice that I missed it sometimes, and her new adventures made our time in Iraq less exciting. She stayed quiet while I filled her in on the everyday drama involved with putting out a weekly paper. Great, more guilt about not listening to her.

She must have considered my life mundane, but she always promised to drive out to my old country house in her BMW Z4 coupe. She loved fast cars.

Chantrea continued explaining to me all the other activities I could do with just one more week in Miami. I nodded and half-smiled when she suggested more shopping adventures. I had already had my lifelong lesson in haggling from her the second day I was in the city. I bet the lesson would have saved me a small fortune in the crowded marketplace outside the Green Zone, but like a typical American, I was embarrassed to barter. Concepcion explained the real social crime was not bartering, and the American way was offensive to the shop owners. What else was new? Americans being offensive abroad was part of our very existence.

I could technically stay if I wanted. The editor of the paper considered me financially as a freelancer, and the fact that I hung around the office was my own choice. I wanted to work in the darkroom and surf the internet. This gave me a reason to wake up and have a purpose. I lived about ten miles from civilization.

"I might stay," I whispered, aware of how quiet my voice had become. I repeated myself loud enough for Chantrea to hear me.

"That's good," she said. "Now you can have a real break. What's in Missouri anyway?"

"My family."

This question was not uncommon for anyone along the coasts of the United States.

"Well, that's a good reason, but I am sure your family wouldn't mind you having a nice vacation in Florida," She emphasized the word *Florida*, as if to remind me she lived in paradise compared to all Midwesterners.

My mind wandered to Chantrea and her idea of family.

Concepcion hadn't told me much about them besides how they'd parented her. I wanted Chantrea to continue our pleasant conversation.

"How did you and Jimm end up in Florida? From

Cambodia, right?"

"Oh, that's a long story. It's a hard one, too." She paused, contemplating something. "What do you know about my country?"

"Not much. I remember the location because of the acronym TLC—Thailand, Laos, and Cambodia—and a little more from when we studied Vietnam in my training and political science courses," I said. "I have to admit, I was always interested in more recent history."

"Well, I've not been back there; we couldn't go back for the longest time because we are considered political refugees from the war," she said. "Now we can go, but I just don't want to. It's still fresh in my memory what happened."

"What do you mean that you don't want to go back?" I was aware I sounded like an American stereotype, assuming I knew more about the world than I really did.

"It's not like that," With patient eyes, she looked up to meet my gaze then sat on the edge of the bed.

"At one time, US law prevented our return because, for us to enter this country, we had to sign a form that stated if we ever returned to our country, we were in danger of being killed."

"Was it true? Would you be killed?" I asked.

"It was not a matter of if. When my first husband

was killed, I knew I had to leave," she said. "I met Jimm again. He was a colleague of my first husband, and I stayed with him. His brothers and sisters escaped safely to Vietnam, but we were still there while the killing of our kind continued."

"Our kind?" I'm sorry, I don't understand. Was there an invading army or something?"

"No, the government, the Khmer Rouge, killed the intellectuals, the professors, bankers, lawyers, anyone who was smart enough to overthrow them."

"So they killed smart people?"

"Yes, and what happened in my country changed the definition of genocide. I looked up more about it when I came here in a book about the man who created the term, Raphael Lemkin," she said. "He was a Polish Jew during World War II and a professor. I think he is one reason I kept teaching. It was the bravest thing I could do, even in a place like America. They made me hate my own education during the war, the fact that I was not ignorant. I never wanted to feel like that again."

"Why target the educated?"

"The Khmer Rouge regime came to power after the US-backed government was defeated. It took five years of civil war, but once they made it there, they decided to get rid of all who opposed their version of socialism. I was educated at an American school through secondary school and even went to dinner as a small child with my dad to visit the American ambassador John Dean. My father was well known in the academic community. You ask why target the educated. With all of my schooling, I understood how fragile power was, and if we remained, we would rise up and fight Pol Pot for our ideals. It was a long campaign of brainwashing, but the smartest ones tried to play ignorant or tried to take on jobs like a taxi driver and claim ignorance at all times about anything else."

I nodded and shifted my weight. I didn't know this history. How much had I missed from Chapa? Why didn't she ever explain this to me?

"Disloyalty was a big thing. If you were in the military in my country, Pol Pot killed all of them early on. My brother was killed in the worst way, like cattle lined up for slaughter. We were dumb, though on some level, we understood. We thought he was a soldier; they killed the soldiers only. But then more people were disappearing, and almost all of my teachers were gone. No one was safe, especially those who worked for Americans."

"How did you leave?" I asked.

"It's hard to explain because I really don't know who told who about us, but we owe this government our lives. They took a risk, and some good people helped us get away," she said.

"Can you tell me more?" I wanted to tread lightly. I wasn't sure how painful this was for her to speak about. My arm tingled.

"More is not so important," she said. "We asked Concepcion not to choose a life that could mean war, yet it may already have been chosen for her."

She was telling me something without directly saying it. I had to know more.

"What do you mean, it was chosen for her?"

She sat for a minute, quiet, with a face that betrayed her. She was working out something in her head.

"She's gone, so it's not as important for me to keep a secret," Chantrea said. "I have not spoken about it with anyone but Jimm, so it's harder to say than I thought."

"What could be harder than what you already told me about Cambodia?"

"Later, after we left Cambodia, Jimm worked on behalf of your government in Vietnam, a secretive unit, one that we don't talk about," she said. "Concepcion's parents shared an apartment with us. They took a chance and helped us come here. My whole family was killed, from what I understand. I built a new one. I didn't want to be around former Khmer Rouge people. Even if they did nothing, most people survived because they were loyal during that time. Many of the good ones died."

"I don't know much about them, and I didn't know they worked for the government,"

This changed everything. A family legacy explained so much about how Concepcion carried herself. Was that why she worked for the FBI?

"You won't find them in any record books," She smoothed out a shirt. "That is something Clara, her mother, told me. It is not in our nature to ask a lot of questions like you Americans do. We accepted what they offered—a new life here. In that region, it was more dangerous for them than it was for us."

For the first time since the funeral, I saw tears in her eyes. She pulled out a handkerchief from her pocket and dabbed her eyes.

"We miss them all," Chantrea said. "Especially Concepcion."

She smiled through her tears then continued. "After Concepcion was born, Jimm and I went to the church for her christening. We accepted the offer of being her godparents. Her parents were both so full of life and gusto—that's the right word, gusto. Concepcion had other family, but her parents wanted us to take care of her in case of their death. We were humbled by the choice. There is too much sadness sometimes, so much tragedy no matter where we live in this world."

"When did you stop working for the government?"

The question surprised her, and she wiped her eyes. "Oh, right after we came here. There wasn't any need anymore. The wars were ending, and no one wanted to talk about all the loss anymore. We were two of many."

Yes, I acknowledged the tragedy, but it also made connections in my mind about Chapa's family and how they disappeared after working in secretive units for the good of the country.

The conversation with Chantrea gave me a bitter taste in my mouth. As my mind took it all in, I couldn't stop the tears. I wanted to acknowledge the Cambodian victims, those who had to live in a world with that reality.

I let the tears flow and listened in reverence. I thought of a million Concepcions, friends, mothers, fathers, children, and the extreme sense of loss overwhelmed me.

I knew it was not so different from what I had experienced with my friend's death.

Jimm and Chantrea survived; they had the will in them to give my friend a home, a family, and stability. When they were my age, they were struggling to simply live. In school learning about the Holocaust, the diary of Anne Frank, and the genocide of eleven million people was part of the curriculum. It was something, as a child, I could not grasp. Reading about Anne Frank had influenced me by adding a human voice to the tragedy.

Years later, at the Holocaust museum in Washington, DC, as a soldier in training, I had stood in a room full of shoes. Shoes of the people whose lives had ended up as a number that was too big to imagine. Those shoes were very real. Small dress shoes for someone like Anne Frank to walk down the cobblestones of her European streets, or large men's shoes that were worn through the soles from a hard day. I had considered genocide a closed chapter in history and thought it wouldn't happen again. I learned later that it kept happening all over the world, and one of the survivors sat in front of me. It had happened here with the Native Americans being slaughtered for their land, or in Iraq when Saddam Hussein had decided to gas his own population, the Kurdish. It was ugly, and there would never be enough tears.

I considered why Concepcion hadn't spoken more about politics with me. Maybe it was because she understood more about it in her own life than I could ever study in a book.

For the past six months, I was numb. I wanted the tears to drip down my face, onto my skin, and shake me loose from the foundation of what I had built in survival mode. I hoped this strength would last at least through the week. I would visit a few more places to remember my friend. If Chantrea could remember and live on to tell of the cruelness of man, then I could live on to tell the story of my battle buddy. The more I learned about Chapa and her family, the more I was convinced she couldn't be gone. It was too simple somehow. I couldn't accept she was dead.

Chapter Nine

I wore my most professional outfit for my visit to the FBI office building where Concepcion worked for a short time. The shape of my long legs was completely covered in wide-legged black pants. I wore a purple short-sleeved, buttoned-up, collared shirt, with my long dark hair pulled back from my face in an Army-regulation-approved bun.

With any amount of exertion, I could start to sweat in the Miami sun. My black leather shoes were basic and boring, but heels were a further distraction with my long frame. It was just plain cruel to wear heels around my vertically challenged friends. They were usually saved for those rare occasions when my two sisters were around, and we would compete for two things, best shoes and smallest waist. I was sure with my latest shopping trip in South Beach, I had my police officer and social worker sisters beat for Christmastime.

Driving in downtown Miami was difficult, but I had seen worse. Chantrea's Honda Civic was just the right size to cruise around the town. The ride was smooth, and between stoplights, I switched the radio stations until I finally found something with a tropical beat.

At least in most places in the US, scanning for potential threats was second to enjoying the diversity of vehicles on the road. I flashed to her funeral and remembered that traffic accidents could happen anywhere, at any time, no matter how engrossing the cityscape became.

I felt a sharp pain in my stomach and wondered if I should turn around and cancel my appointment with Special Agent David Aquila, Concepcion's supervisor.

Chantrea had given me another contact, an Italian-sounding name, but I felt it was better to let the commander know who was in his territory. This saved the endless reintroductions to who I was and why I was there. I wasn't exactly sure what my expectations were of the work, but Chantrea was insistent I visit.

Concepcion's story had been written with a terrible

ending. Maybe I could learn more about her time after we parted ways. I thought of her aunt, who seemed to only remember the teenage version of Concepcion. That was a shame. What if I was judged solely by those years?

Something about this town, this air, made me feel a little more adventurous and spontaneous. I walked through the halls decorated with hotel-room-like artwork and a bright blue shade of shag carpeting, not what I was expecting in a federal office. This was a city with a love of vibrant colors. The floor should be arrested. I guessed they rented the building or had moved in as is. I found the entrance quickly, off to the left. The right side of the building appeared to have other government offices, separated in the long hallway by glass doors with white lettering details.

Opening the door, I could see a petite twentysomething posted at the front desk. She had a pleasant smile plastered on her face. She wore her curly hair short, and her light brown eyes lit up when she saw me. I wasn't sure if they received many visitors.

Miss Luanne Joplin was stenciled into the nameplate on the front of her gray modular desk. Joplin, just like the city. I had won a beauty pageant in Joplin, Missouri, as a child. She probably wouldn't know what I was talking about if I mentioned it.

She kept smiling as she looked me over and over. "You must be Ms. McCoy," she said. "Let me just ring back and let them know you're here."

Them. Who was them?

"We know she's here. We heard the door." A male voice carried throughout the office.

I quickly visualized that this was a small setup, maybe enough space for three or four cubicles. It was different than what I had anticipated when I heard the letter acronym. The man who spoke came into view, rounding the secretary's desk, and offered me his hand.

I grabbed it and looked him square in the eyes, as I had with generals, ambassadors, and lowly privates alike; it was one way to gain respect and to judge how the conversation would go. A limp handshake from the other person was a sure sign of weakness, in the military or in an office with shag blue carpeting.

I took in his deep green eyes, which had a golden ring of fire set in their centers. I instantly knew a strong gaze had been a mistake on my part. His eyes were so beautiful I didn't notice he was shaking my hand off. I had the weak grip today.

I stepped back and asked in a small voice I didn't recognize, "Special Agent Aquila?"

"No, ma'am, I'm not that tan, am I?" I drank in his amazing lean body, arms corded with muscles. He was dark skinned like a Latino, with what my mother would call a Roman nose. She was an expert on attractive men. My own father was no schlub in the looks department, even with a farmer's tan.

"He's actually my boss, kind of. He's mostly based out of the central office, and we get a temporary place to work while they're remodeling." He smiled and gestured toward the floor. Good looks and a sense of humor.

"He rarely comes here, so we can get into all kinds of trouble. I'm sure you want to meet everyone," he pointed to no one. "First, I am Agent Gianni Catanese, and I worked closely with your friend, Agent Concepcion Chapa. Her former partner is now my partner. He's out of the office right now. He would kill me if he didn't get to meet you." He smiled again with his one-hundred-watt smile. That was a lot of information.

"I spoke with Agent Aquila, and he said he would meet me here," I said. "Do I need to go down to the central office?"

"He says a lot of things, but he called Luanne to let her know you were coming. He was busy and thought it was best that we meet."

I nodded, trying to picture Concepcion in this office, working next to a Greek god every day.

"How about we sit in the conference room and wait for Manny Valderron to come back. I can make you a coffee or something, a coconut water or juice."

He bent over the small fridge jutting out from the wall. I looked at the rear view of this sexy man, and I could see the outline of his wallet in the dark denim jeans.

That was a handful I wanted to grab. Concepcion would agree. In fact, she might have even grabbed it for herself. I was smiling on the inside, thinking about her appreciation for certain men, happy I was here. He turned around with two glasses of Pellegrino water with slices of lime inside.

He gave me a knowing smile as he placed the glasses on the table in the room adjacent to the break room. "How do you like Miami?"

"It's growing on me," I responded after an extended pause to think. "I like the shopping, but I hate the traffic."

"Yeah, you're probably not used to all this, being from Missouri and all."

He considered my eyes, and I couldn't tell if he was making a joke at my expense or not. He had a slight smile on his face.

"Oh, I've seen a lot worse, even if I am from a small town," I replied. "I take it you think we're all hillbillies and inbreds who have nightmares about being in the big city."

I changed my voice to have a slight twang for my best hillbilly, inbred impression. Some stereotypes were appropriate, just not for me. I reasoned I was anything but predictable, unless one counted my attraction to this man.

"A lot worse what? Traffic? I suppose you have cities there, too. We have our share of hillbilly types in Florida. We call them rednecks." He paused and looked me up and down. "Though, I am not against the idea of you barefoot and pregnant." He smiled.

My mouth hung open at his comment. I knew he was joking because his eyes changed so slightly. It had been a long while since anyone had openly flirted with me.

"Well, if you like 'em barefoot and pregnant, I can write down some names of my high school classmates who would be happy to oblige you,"

Was I flirting back? I felt my skin flush and my neck break out into red splotches. I hated that my Irish roots betrayed me in my moment of glory. He had me blushing. Now this green-eyed hottie could visually see his effect on me. I felt a little uneasy. I knew nothing about this guy, yet here I was practically throwing myself at him. What would Concepcion say about this?

I would never know.

I needed to pull myself together and get back to the comforts of Jimm and Chantrea's house, pack my bags, and get the hell out of Dodge. Back home, I was safe from feelings of uncertainty.

On the other hand, I still had enough time for a proper adventure.

"So what's on your mind? What do you want to talk about, Miss McCoy?" His smile had faded, and his bottom lip moved over the top lip, like he was considering his next move.

He took in a deep breath. Time was slowing down in the tiny break room of the office. The rise and fall of his chest made me very aware of his magnanimous presence.

I didn't answer. I didn't think I was ready to barrage him with questions. He should be used to it, he was an FBI agent, and I was a journalist. We both had a background with interviews. This wasn't an interview, though. This was just for my own understanding about what had happened to my friend.

"I want to get some air,"

Ever the perfect gentleman, he accompanied me to the front of the building. He appeared to be lost in his own thoughts as he scanned the passing faces of his fellow Miami agents. He sat down on the giant stone steps leading up to the building.

"What was she like as an agent?".

"I can guess you would know. I'm sure she was the same type of agent as she was a soldier," he said. "She was professional, a team player; she had what it takes to be a great agent. She took a lot of risks and didn't take any shit."

Gianni continued for several minutes, talking about my friend, and I started to relax.

I was peeling away the veneer of ignorance about her death. How could a journalist not want to know the full story about her best friend's supposed death? It had been six months, and I hadn't bothered to pick up the phone and ask these questions earlier.

LaLa had tried to excuse my behavior when I asked her about my lack of interest since the funeral. She'd answered, "Everyone grieves in different ways."

Was Valderron involved in her death? Was the man next to me being honest in his description of Concepcion as a good friend? Here was the uncertainty again. My mind was working overtime thinking of all the possibilities.

I guessed working closely with men like Valderron or Gianni would be dangerous territory for a hot, single woman who relied on her job for fulfillment.

"Is Agent Valderron doing okay?"

As soon as the words left my mouth, I knew it was a stupid question. It had been six months, though. Was anyone okay who lost a loved one and/or a partner?

"I'm sorry, I just meant…" I stopped midsentence.

"He will be very happy to meet you and speak with you about Agent Chapa." Gianni shifted his weight, turned to me, and met my eyes. I really wanted to believe those eyes.

"Let's get away from the reason you're here. I don't have a lot of answers. Neither does Valderron," he said, turning serious. "I would keep asking questions, but there is only so much we can tell you. We keep going over the accident, and it doesn't add up."

"What are you trying to tell me here?"

"I'm not sure. For one thing, Valderron and I were called out to Tallahassee at the time of the accident," he said. "We weren't partners at the time, and Agent Chapa was supposed to be home sick."

"Was she by herself?"

"You mean you don't know?" he said. "I was sure Aquila would have told you. He was with her, Joelle. May I call you Joelle?"

I nodded yes.

"They were working some sort of case together, and that is as much as we know. He walked away from the accident without a scratch."

"Was there an investigation? Why don't her parents know anything about this?"

"There was an investigation, but we weren't on the team because we were too close to the victim," he said. "It went on for a few days before it was ruled accidental."

"What does your boss say?"

"He doesn't say anything, and when Valderron confronted him and asked to reopen the case, Aquila threatened to have his badge."

Gianni's face was almost as red as mine. His anger was palpable.

"He can't take his badge, can he? Isn't there an internal investigation unit that can prevent something like that?"

"It's not an idle threat. Apparently, Aquila has been documenting events that make Valderron vulnerable. Almost a year ago, Valderron was involved in a shooting incident with Agent Chapa that some officials call questionable."

"Who shot who?" I was hoping Agent Gianni's sudden urge to tell me the facts would not go away. I was finally getting a few answers, but only thinking of more questions.

"It seems they both shot the suspect, but Agent Chapa's life was threatened," he said. "How could her life be at stake when she shot the suspect first?"

"What does Valderron say?" I tried to conjure the face of Valderron to my memory. Was he a cold-blooded killer?

"He says the suspect was running toward her with a gun, and she pulled her service weapon just in time. The suspect did have a weapon that was later found, but the gun wasn't loaded."

"What happened to them?"

"Nothing. Agent Aquila made all the questions stop and made a convincing case to the investigating agents about the lethality of the man—a real piece of work connected with Miami's underworld and a network of gunrunners."

"If Valderron made a fuss, then Aquila would, what, make accusations about the past?"

"Valderron and Chapa were together, but they weren't out in the open with it," Gianni said. "You have to understand, Aquila can make up any sort of report and Agent Valderron's career is tainted with question marks. Who would take a chance on him after that?"

"If this is an actual threat, then why are you both still questioning the case? If your careers are so important to you, then why risk it?"

"Well, we really hadn't gotten anywhere. Until now," he looked up, his eyes pleading with me. "You might be able to shed some light on something we may have missed."

"Why didn't you call me sooner? I guess you can pick up a phone if you want to find out some information."

"We knew you would turn up soon," he swallowed, revealing a pronounced Adam's apple. "We couldn't risk you talking to Aquila. It had to be on your own terms. You were an unknown to us. You were close to her, yet you didn't stick around for answers. You didn't even pick up the money she left for you. It was like you already knew something we didn't."

"You're wrong, you know, I don't know anything, and I'm as confused as you are," I was unsure of the truth in my answer.

"Then why didn't you come here sooner? She called you her battle buddy, and that means more than her lover or her closest friend."

Battle buddy. It had been a while since I was called a battle buddy.

"I don't have an answer for that. I'm not just here for money. I'm ready to find out the truth about her life here."

"Well, get in line," his tone had more than sarcasm in his voice—anger.

He checked his cell phone and started punching

buttons. I watched an older lady in platforms and a sundress walking her dog. Her arm bangles draped her tiny wrist. She had a style about her that made me think of our administrative assistant back home. Three more just like her came up with their similar small dogs, and I saw that this was a thing here. Being seen and showing off one's walking-teddy-bear canines.

"Have you ever been hunting?"

I gave him a quizzical look but accepted the change in subject. "Many times, though I never got anything. I think I just went to make my dad happy. He always wanted a son."

"Have you ever wanted to hunt an alligator?"

"No, can't say that I have."

"There are plenty of alligators here, and some of them have to die. It's overpopulated. If we don't hunt them, they might find their way up to northern states like Missouri. You wouldn't want that, would you?"

"No." I rubbed the back of my neck where I was straining to see his face. What was he getting at with alligator hunting? "Are you asking me to go hunting with you?"

"In a way, I am. I want you to look around a little more. There are alligators here in Miami."

"Am I supposed to feel threatened now?" I said, half joking.

"Not by me. I think feeling threatened is a healthy feeling, though. I'm sure I'm not the only one unnerved by your presence."

"You don't seem unnerved. You seem very self-assured to me."

"That's what you think," Gianni stood up. He extended his hand to help me off the steps.

I was still mesmerized by the continuous dog-walking ladies of the street, a backdrop of the city that demonstrated the need to be seen rather than exercising with pumps on. A man I recognized walked up the stone steps. He paused as soon as he laid eyes on Gianni. He stopped in front of me as I stood up, and he shook my hand a little too strong. His eyes met mine. I looked at the tiny creases around his brown eyes…kind eyes. No trace of an alligator here.

"I'm sorry I'm late. Did I miss anything?" Valderron said.

"Nothing much. Gianni here gets right to the heart of things. Nice to meet you, Agent Valderron. I'm Joelle."

"I saw you at the funeral, but I was pretty messed up. You can call me Chuey or Valderron. Whatever you like. Concepcion called me by my last name," Valderron said, with a note of sadness in his voice.

"I just broached the subject of our late friend,"

Gianni said. "I wanted to wait for you to question her properly. We were just getting to know each other."

They both stared at each other a moment. Something silent passed between them.

"Let's go inside and get out of this heat," Valderron said.

He extended his arm and motioned us inside the building. He was carrying something, a small book of some kind. I remembered the red cover because I had one just like it at home. Concepcion and I were scrapbooking enthusiasts. Valderron held a book to his chest as we stepped into the elevator. My face flushed, aware of Gianni's eyes on me. My thoughts were back in Iraq, where most of the photos came from. As strange as it seemed, those were happier times.

Concepcion and I had ordered the materials for the scrapbooks from a website with every felt sticker known to man. We found mini soldier girls. They looked so cute in their little uniforms. There was nothing like the reality of working twelve- to fourteen-hour shifts and wasting your youth in a desert on guard duty. I closed my eyes and could see the unfinished book on the floor of our room, Concepcion cutting our photos into hearts, stars, and other shapes.

I guessed Gianni and Valderron had already pored over the immaculate pages of funny photos and memorabilia. I wondered if they'd signed the log we had titled "Official Army Record" in the back of the book.

Once inside the office, I saw Luanne had left for the day. Funny, I hadn't seen her pass by us on the steps. It felt empty, but what did I know. I noticed cameras in the hall outside the office door. I hadn't noticed them before.

Did anyone watch the footage of who entered and left the agency? Security did seem lacking from the outside.

I blinked into the face of the camera; neither Valderron nor Gianni took notice.

It seemed like only minutes since I was last in the break room. I grabbed a water from the refrigerator, not waiting for either man to serve me. I wanted to examine their evidence about Concepcion's death more than an old scrapbook, but they had waited long enough for me to get here. I wouldn't rush them.

How long would I have waited if I were in their shoes? My girlfriend dies suddenly, and I'm waiting for an old pal to come and break open the case.

"Here." Valderron handed the book to me. "I thought you would want this, so I went back to my place. I don't want to hang on to any more than I have to."

"Thank you." I took the scrapbook and a longer look at Valderron.

He was lean and compact. Small compared to Gianni. He wasn't quite handsome, yet he was attractive. It could be the whole package of a young FBI agent who dressed like he was on *CSI* instead of a DC clone. I thought about the men Concepcion had met in the Green Zone, her first contact with the agency. I couldn't remember their faces, just that one had worn a Hawaiian shirt like we were all on some exotic vacation instead of in a war zone. The callousness of the shirt choice pissed me off, but Concepcion did not subscribe to my feelings. She wanted into the FBI.

"Well, you got in, didn't you," I examined a photo of our smiling faces relaxing on an overstuffed couch in the recreation center.

"Excuse me?" Gianni asked.

"Oh...just thinking out loud," I said, hoping he wouldn't ask more questions. I had copies of all these photos. She had insisted on me keeping them. I had a bad habit of throwing things out, and she didn't trust me to take care of them like she would. She was right. I used to have stacks of photos still in the envelopes they were printed in.

During our time on deployment, I made three nice scrapbooks along with her. I made one for my grandma to show off to her political friends. The third book was given as a gift to my local VFW, who raised money and sent us care packages every couple of months. The Ladies Auxiliary took charge of it, and I counted on the book remaining in their archives for future generations to look back on. Yes, a whole generation of female soldiers contributing to another pointless war.

I was proud of my service in a general way, but the devil was in the details. Despite my best judgment, I had read the Bush Doctrine and the countless journalistic accounts of what went wrong.

I ran my fingertips over Concepcion's handwriting, an elegant cursive to my chicken scratch. The pages felt heavy with fingerprints. The book had been handled many times since I had last laid eyes on it. I looked over my shoulder where Valderron was standing above me. The pain on his face was evident. She was his woman. It was hard for him to give this piece of her up.

"You don't have to give this to me," I said. "I appreciate it, but I don't want to take anything away from you."

He looked away. "Please take it, Joelle," he whispered. "I can't hold on to it anymore."

I slipped the book into my handbag.

"I still have her clothes," he said. Hearing his voice change felt like he was committing to his sadness. "I still have everything. It's too much stuff to hold onto."

"Do you want me to help you go through it? I can do that. It's the least I can do. I bet Chantrea and Jimm would help, too."

"Let me think about it, please. It's a nice offer, but I don't know if I can let all of her go until I know what happened. Does that make sense?"

"It does," I said. "I don't know how much help I will be, but I am here, whatever that means."

Gianni came back into the room, breaking up the heaviness. "You both look like you're still at her funeral. Do you guys want to get out of here?" Gianni asked. "Let's take her out tonight, man. What do you say, Chuey?"

"Sure, but first I need to go visit someone," Valderron said. "I'll meet you out for dinner later."

I smiled. It was happening a lot more since I met Gianni.

Twenty minutes passed before I was back in South Beach traffic. My mind was racing with everything I had learned from the guys about Chapa's daily life. She couldn't be bothered to get her own coffee, and one of the two guys was diligent in bringing her a Starbucks soy latte. I guessed it was Valderron, but both could recite her precise order by heart. I nodded, but our experiences hadn't involved lattes, so this was something new—something I didn't understand before. She built strong relationships with everyone she met, not just me. I guessed they told me the trivial details because they could not get into specifics about her casework.

When I pulled up in front of Chantrea and Jimm's two-story house in suburbia, I removed the scrapbook from my purse and, out of curiosity, turned to the record in the back of who had viewed the book.

In tiny penmanship, Valderron had carefully written his name in blue pen. Next to it were little lines and slashes, indicating he had viewed this book nearly a hundred times. I sank back into my seat with this knowledge. Concepcion was really gone, and everyone but me had been searching for answers.

I closed the book and held it close to my chest. When I pulled it away, a tiny mini-soldier fell onto my lap. I opened the book to find where she belonged. I stopped turning when I found the home of the sticker. One half of a page was coming apart.

"Rubber cement," I whispered to myself. "That was your dumb idea."

I felt a sticky, rubbery ball binding two pages together. I had missed it the last time I viewed it. There was a photo missing, a photo of us together. I had one just like it at home. We both liked the way we looked in it, so we'd put the photo right in the center of the book. Other pieces looked ready to come off once I peeled the pages free from each other.

I searched my lap and the sides of the car seat, my purse, and in between the crack of the console—no picture.

Did Valderron take it with him? That didn't make sense; he would have his own photos with her, his own memories.

The photo was Concepcion and me in uniform standing next to a palm tree in a small village outside the Green Zone. Why would he take it and then give me the book? Who else would want a photo of us together?

The list of questions swirling around in my brain was only getting longer.

Chapter Ten

After sifting through my recent purchases from a local Miami boutique, I finally selected a peach cocktail dress. When the dress was combined with a blood orange belt, it made me look like I might belong with two handsome men out on the town. Even if it was only a dinner, I wanted to look nice, though I was still thinking about the scrapbook. I wondered if Gianni had seen it—the many shots of me with no makeup on, hair plastered to my head while in uniform. I really did not miss those uniforms. Besides the mall, I stopped and got a fake tan where Chantrea went to get her hair done. I couldn't believe the poor woman had to airbrush naked, pale tourists for a living. I tipped her an extra twenty dollars simply for having to ask me to lift my leg to spray my bikini line.

Once I was sufficiently primped and beautified, I buzzed around the city and followed the GPS to The Spot, a Mediterranean fusion restaurant. Whatever that meant.

The restaurant was busy, and among the throng of people at the bar, I could make out my two dinner companions. I hoped they had a table lined up because I was not sure I could stand for long in my extremely sexy but not practical stiletto heels. As soon as Gianni saw me, he grinned—a kid in a candy store—and walked toward me.

"Wow, you look great." He greeted me with a kiss on each cheek. I inhaled the scent of him on the second kiss. I was hooked. His smell was intoxicating.

"I wasn't sure I'd make it with all the traffic and these heels, but I've survived worse." I laughed nervously, hoping my face didn't turn red again.

Valderron gave me a toothy smile as he lifted his glass from the bar. "Thank you for having dinner with two *federales*."

"You don't look very federal to me," I said. He didn't; he looked even more coiffed than I had seen him earlier.

We spent the evening talking about family, the

military, the agency, and our friend.

"I have a question about the scrapbook," I said during a lull in the conversation.

"Shoot," Valderron said.

"Did you happen to take a photo out of it? It's okay if you did," I asked.

"No, I looked at them too many times to count, but I didn't take anything," he said.

I believed him because that was my first thought, too. I turned to Gianni. "What about you?"

"Truthfully, I only saw the book once when Concepcion brought it in one afternoon," he said.

Damn, they both looked convincing.

As we spoke, I barely noticed the server eyeing us for occupying the table for so long, but I did see the questions in Valderron's eyes. I could not remember a time when I had smiled so much with two people I had just met. Once there was nothing left to consume, we walked outside into the nightlife of Miami. After Valderron left, I waited nervously for Gianni to invite me somewhere else. I wasn't ready to end the evening so soon.

"How about you come dancing with me?" he asked after what seemed like an eternity.

I would agree to almost anything with Agent Gianni Catanese involved. My skin flushed around him.

"Dancing sounds fun," I replied, searching my purse for a stick of gum; it almost gave me an excuse to answer without looking him in the eye and making a fool of myself.

"Great, I know a place that plays the best salsa and reggaeton until the sun comes up, if your legs can last that long."

Two hours later, I was drinking in the neon flashing lights of the pulsating Latin club whose name I had forgotten two mojitos ago. I continued teasing him with my hip movements and working my ass like I was a Brazilian showgirl against his leg.

I would not act or dance this way if I were back home in the small dance halls of Missouri. These were the moves Concepcion had taught me, which I had perfected in the comforts of my own home. I never dreamed I would put my lesson to use with this man in Miami. Everything was faster here, and after a day like today, I was adjusting to my surroundings.

He was handsome by all standards. There was something about the way he carried himself that made me long to please. I hoped my instincts were right and he was feeling the same way.

My body shuddered as he placed his hands on my hipbones and guided my backside into him. He led me around the dance floor in a way that showed he was a skilled dancer.

On the way to the club, Gianni told me he had taken salsa dancing lessons for several months. The lessons had paid off.

I understood the basic routine but lacked the knowledge of certain more complicated steps. My favorite songs were the reggaeton ones because they let me use my Latin steps and my booty-shaking moves. I didn't think I looked like a farmer's daughter tonight. The pace of the songs kept me wanting more, and I could not tell where one song ended and the next began.

The dance floor was so packed with couples that I did not see the usual awkward crowds of girls or guys standing along the wall that surrounded every club floor I'd seen before. This club was all about two people dancing, and it looked like everyone came with a partner in mind. I questioned Gianni's pick of such a romantic style of getting to know each other at first, but then I remembered it had been two years since I'd had a man so close to me. Gianni wasn't just any man. We were both adults.

I sensed Gianni examining my face, hinting at something he wanted to say or perhaps do. I leaned in and brushed my lips against his, testing the waters for a kiss and inhaling his scent. He kissed me hard on the mouth, taking my teasing mouth and making it his.

Then I felt his touch. He was still grinding against me, holding my head in his hands. Before I could break the kiss and breathe, I felt his tongue opening my lips. He wasn't letting me go. I heard him take a breath through his nose. *Yes, yes, yes.* I was sure my body was crying yes as well. He finally released my lips, leaving me to relax against his chest. I looked over his shoulder and saw other like-minded couples dancing to the Puerto-Rican reggaeton beat pulsating around us. No one had noticed us; I loved that. It made me feel like we belonged together, at least in this moment. Everything else be damned.

After a few more pheromone-induced turns around the dance floor, Gianni suggested we get out of the club. Our kisses were full of passion, and after a long night of making out in his car, I was too tired to push for more. I could blame the alcohol or the heat, but I wanted at least one night in his bed. He walked me to the door, and as I pulled out my spare key set, he whispered in my ear, "How about lunch tomorrow?"

"Well, how about dinner instead?" I countered.

My reasoning being that I needed my beauty sleep. Actually, I needed more than sleep, but I wasn't going to give away all my secrets. I wanted to have a whole day to find something to wear. If I could, I would put the night on repeat and hope for a different ending.

"Whatever the lady likes," he said, emphasizing the word *lady*. "It is the least I can do after I finally found a proper dancing partner. You were amazing. I just knew you would be when I first saw the video of you dancing with your battle buddy."

I was mortified. *That* video? Was there no end to the material Concepcion had left for her friends to find? The footage was a spur-of-the-moment music video fueled by Red Bull and SweeTarts where we danced in a guard shack. It sounded like a good idea at the time.

"What else haven't you told me?" I asked, trying not to laugh, but the question was serious. I punched him in the arm to lighten the mood. He nodded in understanding.

"Well, that is why you're here, for the truth. Why would I tell you? Concepcion said she would introduce us some day and then showed me the video. It hadn't seemed appropriate to mention it until now."

That sounded like Concepcion; she would do that, especially since she was running the camera most of the time while making the video. I recalled a part on the video where I showed her how us farm girls get down. I wore spandex running shorts and pigtails while I danced around. What the hell was I thinking?

He had known I liked to dance, and he wanted me to have fun on one of my last nights there. Somewhere

Concepcion was laughing her ass off. I was sure of it.

"See you tomorrow, and this time I get to pick where we go.".

"How could you possibly know where to go? You're a tourist, and I don't think you should pass up my entertaining abilities." He held the door open for me while he tried to convince me.

"Until tomorrow, Gianni," I wasn't going to let him have the last word. I started walking away but turned back to see him again. He was still standing there, smiling. He leaned in and pulled me to him for a long kiss.

"Goodnight, Joelle."

"Goodnight," I managed after catching my breath. Best date ever.

I crawled into the queen-size bed in the guest room at Jimm and Chantrea's house. I was still grinning like an idiot. I hadn't been kissed like that ever. It wasn't only a physical response; my mind was reeling from the constant back-and-forth between us. I had to have him. I pushed the thoughts about Concepcion's death out of my head. Instead, I fell asleep thinking the most embarrassing thoughts about a completely sexy FBI agent.

The next afternoon, I finally woke up to Chantrea working in the laundry room. I made myself get up even though I wanted to lie in bed until my dinner date. I needed to stretch my legs, which were sore from the hours of dancing in heels. I remembered that tonight I had to pick where we would go, and I had no clue where to start. It had been a long time since the options of a date included more than dinner or a visit to the pool hall or going to an ancient, run-down movie theater in my hometown.

I looked through my available wardrobe, hoping to find something that would spark my imagination. In the back of the closet, I noticed an open box with paperback romance novels spilling out of the top. I wasn't really a fan of romance books; I preferred crime thrillers. These must have been Concepcion's from high school. I checked the copyright date, and I was sure. I flipped through the books, worn with creases in the corners. The men on the covers paled in comparison to Gianni. Now, if he were on those covers, I could be persuaded to change genres.

One book stood out from the rest. Blue-turquoise water and a sandy beach covered most of the cover, and on the right-hand side, a couple embraced in the sand, entangled in each other's arms. The beach was where I wanted to go. I picked up the book and put the rest back where I found them in the closet. It couldn't hurt to have a little fantasy reading before my real-life encounter with an FBI agent. I needed a little gumption to ask him while sober to stay the night with me.

I started to imagine Gianni on the beach, the salty water lapping at our feet. Sand in our toes, him on me. I had to consider the consequences; I felt so many emotions while I was around him. What would Concepcion say? She was a believer in carpe diem. I wished I could call her and ask for the kind of advice I wanted to hear. Concepcion was the only woman I knew who did exactly what she wanted to do; consequences be damned.

While I read a steamy scene about a pirate and captain's daughter, I felt something stuck to the back of the book. I turned it over and pulled off a worn-out-looking postcard.

The postcard was from Mendoza, a wine region in Argentina.

Who were Clara and Carlos? It looked at least a decade old. I tried to read the date on the postscript, but it was scraped off. It was to Clara and signed Carlos and written in a tiny Spanish script. Where had I heard the name, Clara? I just couldn't place where I knew that name.

I sat up on the bed, my thoughts far away from the beach and now engulfed in a new mystery.

The card started "*mi amor, Clara,*" but my Spanish

was rusty.

I would ask Valderron to try to translate the card. Maybe he could help me get information and answer the questions we were all searching for. She was his future, and she wasn't here anymore. At best, she knowingly left him.

I still needed to get dressed for my date, but I decided a quick call home might give me the confidence I needed to face Gianni again.

I dialed the number and considered what my seventy-five-year-old spitfire of a grandma was up to at five in the afternoon.

"Hello…" I listened to her southern Missouri drawl and felt instantly at home.

"Grandma, it's Jo. What are ya doing?" All in one breath, my words strung together with the familiarity of her voice.

"Aw, Jo, you called me right when I was cutting into a piece of cake." I heard her take a bite. "Oh, this is good. I picked it up at the bakery. It's buttercream, our favorite. What should we say we're celebrating?" She laughed, a real laugh from her gut, high-pitched. "We're celebrating your phone call. Is that good enough?"

"Of course it is, Grandma,"

"What's new?" she asked. "Are you still in Florida?"

"Yes, I am, but I was calling to bother you. I'm trying to figure out what I'm going to wear."

"Where are you going? Anywhere fun?"

I debated telling her the truth. She knew I rarely went out on dates, and they were usually just to please my mother. On the other hand, Grandma seemed a little more lighthearted in her quest to get me married off.

"Out on a date."

"You are? About time. Well, that just makes this cake taste even sweeter."

I pretended to be jealous, but cake was the last thing on my mind. I filled her in on the highlights of my vacation, and then we got right down to it. After hearing a general description of Gianni in which I found myself uttering the word *beefcake*, Grandma gave some easy advice.

"You only live once, my Jo, so don't wait for him to kiss you again. Sometimes you have to make the first move if you want someone bad enough."

"Is that what you did with Grandpa?" I asked, knowing that after fifty-five years of marriage, I would take most advice from my grandparents.

"Of course I did."

"Is that what you want me to do, Grandma? Run off to Florida and be with a strange man."

"Well, that's not what I said, but you went down to Florida to get your questions answered." Her voice changed to a whisper. "I heard little else about your friend, and I don't think my contacts know enough to help you search more. This is a war on all fronts. I'm just glad you're out of the line of fire."

"You're right," I said. "I'd better go get ready. Give Grandpa a kiss and a hug for me. I love you."

"I love you, too, Jo. You call me again tomorrow, and tell me how it went."

"How what went?"

"Your date, Jo, your date."

"I'll try, Grandma." After our goodbyes, I hung up my cell phone, set it on the bed, and went back to the closet.

I called up the stairs. "Chantrea, can I borrow your makeup?" I used my sweetest tone.

Using the postcard as inspiration, I told Gianni that a picnic on the beach was just what I had in mind.

"The beach it is. I know the perfect spot," he said after only a moment's hesitation.

"Is it where you take all your dates?" I teased, not

quite sure if I wanted to know the answer.

"Only the ones from out of town." He grinned.

I punched his arm in response and saw him smile and lick his lips while he watched the road.

As he drove to the beach, I caught him sneaking peeks at my bare legs exposed in the passenger side. I looked good, but he looked great, too. He had an eye for designer clothes, and he wore them nicely. It was a nice change to be around a man who cared about his appearance.

He wore dark-washed jeans with black Ferragamo Italian leather boots and a V-neck T-shirt that exposed his tanned arm muscles and chest. I didn't know if we were dressed exactly for the beach, and I didn't care. I just wanted to be alone with him. I hadn't thought about Concepcion in almost an hour. That had to be a record while in Miami. Hell, even in Missouri she was still in my daily thoughts.

I had to force myself to breathe while Gianni maneuvered the car throughout various side streets along the beach. I kept thinking about all the ways I could screw the night up. I hadn't been on a date in forever and the whole "wind in the air" might have been a little too romantic. I wanted to get to know everything there was to know about Gianni.

Once we arrived at the beach, I looked around and

saw the parking lot was mostly empty with a few kids' bikes and a motorcycle about a hundred yards away, but I didn't see the owners. It was secluded and private. Perfect spot, indeed.

I reached in the back of his car to grab my purse, and Gianni's hand was on my face, pulling me in for a kiss.

"I wanted to do that all day, and since you got in, I couldn't wait to park it again" His voice husky with desire.

It had been less than twenty-four hours since I first considered having sex with this man. I paused. It was all happening faster when my heart was pounding. The thoughts stopped as his hand touched my ankle, inching its way up my skirt. Control was overrated.

It had been a very long night and day since we had parted.

"This is happening, right?" My chest heaved, hoping my blunt question wouldn't stop the motion of his fingers probing inside me.

"I made up my mind last night that I would be a gentleman. Not take advantage just because you danced like that, teasing the shit out of me," he answered. "These legs, though…the face is not helping me say no plus a smart mouth."

"You're done with being a gentleman?" I arched

my back against the seat. It was good. I closed my eyes. He smelled amazing.

"Oh, I will be gentle." His eyes, half open, pleading with mine beneath long eyelashes. "I want to show you how hard it was for me last night to leave you. Can I be inside you?"

"You're talking too much again. Yes, fuck me," It was hard to think any rational thoughts.

"Not a problem." He kissed me hard on the mouth.

A few seconds later, I was lifted out of my seat by his giant arms, and he put me on his lap. I heard the condom wrapper open but was still in shock over how large Gianni was as he maneuvered the rubber onto himself. It hadn't mattered to me until this moment, but now the thought of his full-length cock inside me made me short of breath.

He had pulled me from the steering wheel, but I could still feel my ass brush up against it as he lifted me up and down on his cock. He pulled me up again and again.

We didn't speak words, but volume was an issue. I hoped any kids belonging to those bikes were far, far away.

Sometime later, we settled down on the shore, and I leaned against his chest. He hadn't let me go for hours now and moved me close to him as the stars brightened the skies.

I heard a group of teenagers come to claim their bikes, and eventually a couple for the motorcycle. I had picked up food earlier at the grocery store where Chantrea shopped. I settled on a meal consisting of chicken bacon wraps, a bag of pita chips, and freshly made hummus. For dessert, I brought an orange and a single serving of carrot cake.

We ate slowly while watching the waves come in. Gianni made me laugh when he decided to feed me the orange.

"These oranges are delicious, so ripe and fresh." They tasted better than anything in our supermarket. "What variety are these?"

"We are in Florida, I think everything tastes better here," he replied. "Probably the same variety you eat in Missouri except without the plane ride. People here are picky about their fruit."

Later, he told me about why he became an FBI agent and about his large family, who originated from the island of Sicily surrounded by the Mediterranean Sea. He talked slow and almost in a whisper. I thought about asking him to come stay with me at my house.

It sounded a little crazy, but after our time in the car, sanity was overrated.

At the end of the night, I crawled into bed and let

out a quiet, but excited, gasp. Little Joelle was a bad girl in a very good way. Definitely couldn't come clean to Grandma about this one, but this was one story I needed my best friend to hear. It wasn't only a physical response to Gianni. My mind was reeling from the constant back-and-forth between us. I now understood why she wanted to set us up.

The prospect of returning home made me genuinely sad, but at least I had this one night to obsess over.

Chapter Eleven

It was a little over a month later when Gianni came to visit me on my farm. We spoke almost daily after I came home, usually in the evening when we could talk well into the night. After our conversations, my cheeks would be tired from laughing and smiling so much. Who knew men like him existed? When Gianni announced he was coming to St. Louis for a work conference, I could hardly contain myself.

I called in my reinforcements to help me prepare the old farmhouse for a visit. I wanted him to like my home because I wanted him to like me. I hoped he could like the life I'd built for myself. It scared me, thinking about something different, something like a Miami condo in a city of two and a half million people.

His plan was to stay for four days after the conference. I channeled all the domestic goddess energy and recipes I could summon and made a point to make him feel welcome in the Show-Me State. It was ironic that I, who thought of myself as an independent, strong woman, was thrilled over taking care of this man. Time flew by, and on the third day of staying around my farm, mostly in my four-poster queen-size bed, we decided to go for a long run.

We started out on the red dirt and gravel road as slow as I could muster. I explained that we had to be on the lookout for two things, snakes and stray dogs.

"So there aren't alligators on their way to this Walmart?" He set his fancy cardio meter.

"What Walmart?" One of the advantages of living in the middle of nowhere meant the nearest discount shopping store was at least forty-five minutes away.

I was looking forward to hearing his labored breath and watching the glistening sweat beads pour from his brow. He smelled so musky and clean at the same time, and when I showered alone, I would breathe in his body wash that sat next to all my girly scents. I was tempted to shower with his stuff just so I could have the scent on me throughout the day. I would wait until he left, however, and hoped I could find his brand at the local drugstore.

Our heavy breathing added to the sounds of the crickets, and the slight breeze set the pace for a good workout. About a half mile into the run, Gianni broke the silence.

"How often do you come out here and run?"

"Almost every night unless I decide to go into town and do a Richard Simmons class at the senior center."

"Seriously? Oh, so you're a Richard fan? Besides hanging out at retirement homes, what else haven't you told me?"

"That I'm glad you came," I said. "I usually play harder to get than this."

On a whim I started sprinting, full speed ahead, hoping he would follow me. He did, and, after several seconds, ended up passing me with his powerful legs pumping hard. I was mesmerized and slowed down. He circled around to meet me.

"You are so hot when your face gets cherry red." He touched my cheek as we both struggled to catch our breath. "Your freckles come out a little bit. It's cute."

"I am not cute." I punched his arm, playfully fighting with him. "I'm hot."

A few hours later, we sat on my overstuffed, chocolate-brown sofa, resting our bodies from the last several days of nonstop activity. He caressed my hair as

I rested my head on his lap. His jeans smelled like my lavender fabric softener.

I felt free, and I hardly recognized myself. There could be happiness out of so much pain. The guilt of that thought remained as I considered what this meant. This was me, living my life, and Concepcion was in harm's way. I hoped she would understand how much I needed him in my life. The same joy I had could be gone as quickly as it had found me. This sobering idea gave me the guts to be happy, as nothing is decided or written in stone.

He broke the stillness of the night and the train of my thoughts. "You are so different than I imagined."

The idea of him imagining me before we met gave me a shiver up my spine. I adjusted my weight and lay back down, wanting to stay close. Right now, being next to him was enough.

One week after I kissed him goodbye at the airport, my world tumbled out of my control once again.

Gianni called me at work to tell me he was being sent away in two months on a special assignment. He wanted me to come stay with him.

"I couldn't tell you last week because it wasn't a sure thing. I know you're still worried about

Concepcion, and I didn't want to bother you."

"Bother me? Why would I be bothered?"

I hung up on him, a hot flush of red filling my face.

My cubicle looked sad suddenly with a slip of paper from a fortune cookie that read "you will find luck in love," a plane ticket stub from Florida, and a photo of my two favorite people, Concepcion and Gianni, together. The picture had been shot in Miami at a co-worker's party, most likely by Valderron. It usually made me smile to think of them in the same place together. Somewhere deep inside me, a tiny voice was saying I told you so.

I could not stomach taking a six-month break with no contact. How could people leave their soul mates once they found them? Whoa. Now I knew I was getting ahead of myself. I never wanted anyone like this. We had almost nothing in common except Concepcion and service to our country. Surely that was enough these days, to have someone who understood what it meant to be in harm's way.

Gianni told me I wasn't like any of the other women he had dated, specifically because I wasn't an FBI groupie or a constant worrier about his choice of career. I didn't ask too many questions because I knew from experience that he couldn't answer most of them. Now I wanted to know, and at the same time, I couldn't know. Not about him, not about her. I had to not ask.

I thought about my own time in the Army. Hurry up and wait, the mantra of the Army. Did that man on the phone just order the butterfly back to its silk wrapping? Could my life become a reed among many, blowing along every which way the wind wanted me? Or would I refuse to bend and break?

I walked out of the office and sat at an empty bus stop, cradling my knees to my chest. I wanted to explode. I wanted comfort. I dialed my little sister's number on the sleek, black Motorola Razor Gianni had bought me. It was identical to his phone. He called it my G-phone, G for government.

She answered on the second ring, just like she always did. Police officers always had to pick up their phones, especially ones who wanted to make detective. I hoped she would know what to do. Who was I kidding? No one could help me. This was what I'd signed up for so many years ago.

"LaLa, you're not going to believe this," I said. "Gianni has to go away for six months, and I can't see him."

"No, Jo. Oh my gosh."

I started to cry with the finality of it all. I was blubbering like a baby, but I needed to let it out.

I needed to call Gianni back.

He was in this with me now.

He answered on the third ring, with a song playing on the radio in the background; he must have been driving.

"Honey, you know that's not how it works. I don't want to sound like a dick, but they're using everyone they have now."

I kept ranting into the tiny phone, letting my worst fears go. Anyone who overheard my side of the conversation would assume I was the biggest whiner on the planet. His own career made him understand about sacrifice. He had to go places he didn't want to go every day.

After my energy was spent, all I could do was cry and choke down my own emotions.

"We will make it through." He said the words that finally eased my sobs.

As a man in law enforcement, he understood the many psychological wounds that came from a life-and-death situation. Though his uniform and responsibilities were very different from my own, there was always the threat of losing oneself to the job, the mission, physically or mentally.

I took his reassurance as a mantra. Something I could repeat to myself, anytime, anywhere I was, next to him or worlds apart. I would do whatever it took to make this work with him. Was he committed like me? Well, only time would tell.

As we continued talking, I started to unclench my hands from around my knees. I sat up a little straighter on the bench. I glanced around the busy street, suddenly aware of myself. I was nearly in the fetal position in full view of the public.

He eventually hung up after many assurances that I was capable of making it back to the quiet comforts of my country home. I simply had to put one foot in front of the other. It sounded easy, but just a few hours earlier, I hadn't been sure I could keep going on. Now I was not taking for granted these small victories. He had me out of myself and out of my crazy thoughts. How was that possible? The strangest thing I had confessed to him during my tirade at the bus stop had to be the idea of him coming back numb, like many veterans of the war. I didn't know what the assignment would hold.

In the dining facility, the emptiness could be found on the faces of countless soldiers of all occupations. I had seen death walking around in people, and it scared me. I recognized my own humanity, and I wanted to hold onto it. Concepcion had once made a joke that only sane people feared ending up crazy.

I'd glimpsed the coldness of that inner death when

I heard my battle buddy had died. It was what I did not do that saved me. I grieved for her, and I was healing. I didn't want to be broken or damaged. I was a coward for getting out while the fighting continued. I wanted to continue being selfish and without the scars of war. Some people never left the wars they fought in, and despite my veteran status, I didn't feel like I really had to fight anyone but the bureaucracy of the unit. I only heard the mortars, but I didn't run from them. The noises of the gunfire and helicopters, these things became common enough to fall asleep to, and the complacency crept in.

On guard duty, I didn't have many close calls, but somehow Concepcion had found herself in the line of fire on a frequent basis. She never spoke freely about all of it, but the talk from our unit was that she was one badass Boriqua and a hell of a shot. It was common for the guys to look past me and go clean their weapons next to her. I was not a real soldier, a worthy soldier, one who deserved everything a veteran's status would bring. I was ashamed to admit that I felt this way, but on those nights when I heard her toss and turn with bad dreams, I asked myself was it worth the cost? I couldn't choose the hard way anymore, enlisting was enough. But unlike me, Concepcion didn't complain; Concepcion thrived.

She always volunteered when it came to our rotation to go outside the wire, and I was happy she accepted. Concepcion and I talked through many of our tough times, thinking we were co-therapists, piloting our sanity. When I was there in the sand, I was comforted by my weapon, my job, the control I thought I had, but now, I was terrified. A sickening feeling about being alone. The weight of the coming decisions hit me.

Though I was usually able to suppress it, I recalled a group of men, fellow soldiers, huddled over a wide-screen laptop and watching video footage of their latest search and seizure. I heard the coldness and cruelty in the way they spoke about the families we were supposed to be protecting. I watched from behind and said nothing. I argued with myself about who was right in the situation; it just didn't feel okay to me, to see this same group trashing a family's home and considering it standard procedure. I was wrong to ask Concepcion about it. It only revealed my naïveté to her about the situation.

It was a numbness I observed as they watched a video of a group of women and children cooking at home when they knocked on the door and burst in. One of those women died that day—someone's grandma, someone's wife, and someone's mother—by being at the wrong place at the wrong time. To the soldier who took her life, she was a potential threat, and the worst part was he'd followed protocol in the situation. What would I have done? In anywhere but war I could say I didn't ask for this, but I signed up for it, not knowing the reality of what that would mean.

Concepcion had explained the situation to me one night like she had a key to a soldier's code that I didn't learn.

"Grandma or not, Joelle, women are killers, too, and they could have easily killed that private if he hadn't acted. We just don't know. You don't understand. They're just doing their job, and someone should do it. We can't leave any stone unturned, not in war. I would have done the same thing, Joelle. I love you, girl, but you weren't made for all this," she had said.

"And you are?" I asked her after a heated argument about the fairness of war.

"I guess I am," she said. "And I am not ashamed of it."

From then on, it would be just plain silly for me to try to be like her, a perfect example of a soldier. She left me sitting on my bed, contemplating the rest of my life without the Army, without her. For the life of me, I could not regret joining, but I wouldn't re-enlist; I would never choose to go back. There was a difference this time, ignorance was bliss the first go around, but this time I knew better than to believe I was a soldier like her.

The phone interrupted my thoughts.

It was my mom.

"Oh, honey. You will just never guess," she didn't give me a chance to answer.

"Mom, I don't want to guess. What's up?" I was aware of the anger in my voice.

"Your cousin Tisha just joined the National Guard right out of high school. She is gonna be a soldier just like you. You should call and give her some advice or something. But, honey," her voice whispered into the phone as if she were telling me a secret, "don't get all down on her with your deployment stuff."

As sarcastically as I could manage, I asked, "Oh, so you want me to lie to her. Well, my mama taught me better than lying."

"Joelle, think of someone besides yourself for once." She sounded pissed off.

After she hung up on me, which was our usual way of communicating, I debated calling my cousin. Oh hell, who was I to rain on her parade? Everyone had to figure it out on their own. I sure did.

A hardness was building inside my chest. I

imagined myself back in the desert, alone and without the freedom to plan my own day, shower by myself, or to find out the truth about Concepcion Chapa.

"Mama, Mama, can't ya see, what this Army's done to me…" I sang under my breath.

Chapter Twelve

The beads of sweat slid down my spine; pooling moisture formed in the crevice of my lower back. I didn't mind. With my head tilted to the side of the pool chair, I watched with amusement as Gianni drained the water bottle I had packed earlier in the day. After every drop was gone, he turned to me and smiled his reassuring smile.

On the top of his Miami condo, I checked myself for any redness and then the clock for how long I had tanned on my back. This was the first time I had a real tan, and it suited me. My long dark hair contrasted against my now brown skin. I was one hot mama. My usually freckled pale skin needed more attention here, but I liked the changes in the mirror.

I shook off the sweat and turned to face him, no small feat with my swimsuit top barely hanging on.

The threat of his departure seemed a world away. We'd spent a couple of months together, but I was closer to him than any other man I'd dated. He was the only person I wanted to give in to my intimate sexual desires with. Relaxing with him was exactly what I needed because, after two previous tours of duty, the hurry up and wait mentality for the inevitable was not possible when I had to be strong for my own sanity.

Fidelity wasn't hard for me, but I'd had to witness how many of my fellow unit members cheated, and I was disgusted. This fact might have led me to overcompensate with my time left with Gianni. We shed our own weight in sweat from making love in the Miami heat. I coached myself daily to live in the present. I would need good memories to fuel the next six months apart. I was ready for anything with him

"Come here now and spend the time you have left with me. I can't think of us being apart when we know what comes next," he had said. I'd booked my ticket before self-doubt crept in and ruined my chance at love.

While I toweled myself off, I thought about what I should make for dinner. Everything involved the grill, and I was even losing a few pounds.

"Honey, what should we make for dinner?" I asked. "I was thinking shellfish…"

He sat on the lounge chair and pulled me onto his lap. "Miami looks good on you," he whispered as he kissed my neck. I felt his hands on my bikini bottoms.

"Are you sure this is a good idea?" I closed my eyes, feeling his kiss, and trying not to focus on the semipublic display we were putting on.

"Don't worry about our neighbors. We're alone."

His fingers traced the inside of my thigh and spread my legs a little wider. Just the way he said, "our neighbors" was incredibly hot. We were together, and nothing could undo the rightness of this moment.

After a long, lazy nap, Gianni and I made our way to the grocery store on a mission for shrimp kabob ingredients, a pineapple, and Greek yogurt. I wanted to grill the pineapple, too, and dip it in the yogurt like I'd seen on *Rachael Ray*. The other not so good thing about a two-month vacation was I had a lot of time to waste while Gianni went into the office. I watched plenty of daytime television with my grandma on the phone. She was happy to share her opinion on the best of daytime TV with me.

One day she heard she could change her life with flaxseed oil and wheatgrass. That afternoon, she called to tell me she'd bought everything on the list except for the wheatgrass.

"Now, what I want to ask Dr. Oz is how am I supposed to afford food?" she said. "I bought all those vitamins, and now I don't have any money left for the rest of the stuff. Why is grass so expensive anyway?"

For some reason, things like grocery shopping were more exciting than I remembered. A necessity of life became fun. I usually hated grocery shopping, but with Gianni, I felt like a kid: racing down the aisles, buying products we didn't have in my town's grocery store. I loved the way he teased me when I picked out items that didn't match the list, and it made me even more spontaneous.

"What's on your mind, babe?" He drove home, picking up on the fact that my head was full of unspoken thoughts.

"I was just thinking of how nice it is being here with you," I said. "Even if we're stuck in traffic."

We weren't hurried in our time together, but the rest of the world kept turning around us. I didn't enjoy thinking about the immediate future.

Our conversations consisted of the present, not the inevitable after when we would be separated.

As I watched out the window, my face relaxed into a smile thinking about our time together. Instinctively, I checked my arm for any hint of sun damage. As a typical pale-skinned eighteen-year-old private, the drill sergeant had made it very clear to me that I was not allowed to get a sunburn, or I would be punished with an Article 15, which meant destruction of government property, and it usually resulted in paperwork and extra duty. I was free to sunburn or tan now. I wanted to stay that way with every fiber of my being.

It was risky spending all my time with Gianni before he left; my parents hadn't quite understood the urgency. How could they? I had never been serious about anyone romantically before.

It made me proud and acutely aware of how fast we were moving. Maybe this separation was a good thing? It could put the brakes on it or be what we needed to test the weight of our relationship. Just enough pressure to push us together or break us apart. I hated to think like that because I felt ashamed. But how long would I have held Gianni at arm's length, working out my own trust issues in the tiny town I had made my home? How long would I have lived half a life, content to hear his voice on the phone and spend one weekend a month with him and then come back to the reality of living alone? Our vacation type of romance got a big fucking wake-up call by way of the Federal Bureau of Investigation. This wasn't the first person the FBI was taking away from me.

Gianni said little as the time got closer, but he made love to me with an increasing urgency. About three days before he was supposed to report for duty, I could tell something was weighing on his mind. His face would change suddenly when I brought it up. At times, he acted like he was privy to something I was not, his eyes flashing with an unsettling knowledge.

Later that night, I knew something was up. The man could truly break me in an instant. That was dangerous territory for a small-town Missouri girl.

My own career as a soldier and part-time journalist stuck in my head. Being with this accented stranger in sultry Miami was the biggest adventure of my life, and this included many big-ticket items such as learning to comfortably sleep near an M16 with gunfire in the distance and holding my sister's hand while she went through labor with my first niece. Just witnessing my own humanity that close had made me a lifetime believer in God Almighty. My life was more out of my hands than I thought.

These feelings came to mind when Gianni

proposed something to me that I truly did not expect. After dinner at a local seafood restaurant, where I ate two lobster tails and had a very alcoholic strawberry margarita, Gianni pulled the car over.

"Joelle, there is something I need to ask you." His eyes met mine. He looked nervous, worried, and even a little frightened. Was I that scary to speak to? My hands started to shake underneath his grasp. I looked outside. Just where in the hell were we if he proposed marriage? I had to remember every detail for future reference.

I swallowed hard and managed to squeak out a reply. "Go ahead, ask me."

"Do you trust me?" he was serious.

A little taken aback, I straightened my outfit and thought about the question just briefly enough. "Yes, I trust you."

"Good, because what I'm about to tell you will seem strange at first, but I have to tell you something."

What the hell was going on with him? I hadn't seen him this ominous before. We had just spent nearly two months talking about practically our whole lives. I hoped my trust was well placed.

"Joelle, I can make it so I don't have to leave. I mean, with my contacts, I can make it happen." He paused long enough for me to interject.

"I'm listening…"

"We have some strings we can pull, but I have to tell you that this would mean you would be unable to go home. Well, at least not right away."

My mind began to race at the picture he was painting. Returning home was not my biggest priority now.

"What would I do instead?" I was still trying to understand what this would mean.

"I can't explain right away, but I can tell you that you will be working with me on a very serious case. Something which you're already involved in"

I watched him as he explained. It was not my boyfriend; this was a cold-hearted agent. Even his voice had changed since the sweetly laced "do you trust me" had passed over his lips just a few minutes before.

Sensing the change of tone, I stopped feeling hopeful and started getting pissed. I brought my finger beneath his chin and pulled his face close to mine. "Gianni, don't play with me. I'm serious. What case are you talking about? When did I become involved?"

He jerked away from me and started the car. "I can't answer those questions now because it will only make you upset, and we can't risk that. You'll understand everything tomorrow."

"Then why bring it up? Now you made me confused and pissed. I hope that's what you wanted. I cannot be Miss Nice Joelle until I understand what's going on. I wish you'd just tell me."

"Stop, just stop. You don't understand. If you leave now, you will ruin everything for us and for someone you really love. Months of investigation. It is someone you would do anything for." His eyes pleaded with me; I couldn't look away. "Please don't leave."

Why couldn't he just say her name? It had to be Concepcion, but he was acting like we had a bug in the car or something.

"What choice do I have? I trust you. But, more than anything, I want to get out of this car. I want to be back in control of this situation that is my life. You can't play God with a person's life, Gianni. The military already did that to me, so don't be confused when I don't allow others, even you, to try to follow suit. Who do you know, excluding yourself, that I would do anything for? I am not going to quit asking until you tell me."

He started driving, paying extra attention to following all traffic regulations. I doubted he would relent and tell me anything.

Gianni stayed silent the rest of the way to his condo. My mind was turning now. How had this night changed from a possible marriage proposal to a damn near threat about some unknown person? Just as he pulled into the garage, it came to me.

Concepcion wasn't my first thought nowadays. It had been a long year since her disappearance and over two since I'd laid eyes on her. I was there, in Miami, and I wasn't visiting anyone that related to her but Gianni.

"Concepcion, that's the only person we both have in common. This is about my battle buddy. It's her," I practically shouted into his ear.

"Shut up, okay, just shut up. Don't talk to me about something I can't explain now."

And for the first time since we started the conversation, I saw a flicker of emotion in his eyes. His voice was harsh in his throat and sounded like he smoked a pack of cigarettes in the meantime. Scratchy and raw. Was he crying? Maybe he was, but I needed answers, and for damn sure I didn't need the strongest man I thought I would ever meet to start coming apart at the seams.

"Fine, tell me when I can know because I can't stay here with you, wondering what other trapdoor you're going to open up. What is so important about tomorrow?"

"It's when Chuey gets back. It isn't just about us, Joelle. I wish it was, but it's not. I can't be the one to give you all the information, and tomorrow is the first opportunity we have."

"How long have you known that this assignment was optional? Better yet, how long have you been hiding this case from me?"

He looked away in silence then filled in a few of the blanks I had about the story.

"I won't ask again; just tell me. I can't even grasp what tomorrow will bring, but I know I have fallen in love with you, and I deserve to know if you have some other motive than just being with me."

"I won't lie." He was the one giving the eye contact now. This was an FBI agent. This wasn't my lover. "I wasn't sure we could swing it before today. It could still fall apart, but I wanted you to know as soon as I found out. We need to find answers, and we need your help. I can't be your confidant right now. I need to ask for something that may break us up."

I didn't know what to say, so I stayed silent. Was I being investigated for something by my boyfriend? Was I an assignment for him? I was supposed to be the one searching for answers about my friend, not the one being surveilled.

I took note of the way my body was reacting to the news. My hands were clammy and warm despite the cold air, and my face was no doubt flushed. Like clockwork, when I got nervous or drank a little too much alcohol, my neck would break out into red uneven splotches. This was one of those times. All I could feel was my stomach turning and twisting into emotional knots. My heart was beating far too fast. I honestly couldn't think of what to do next. I did not want to be with him tonight, but being alone in a hotel wasn't what I wanted either. Before I had a second to reconsider, I knew where I should go, the only place I could go in this city.

"Take me to Jimm and Chantrea's house. I don't want to stay with you for obvious reasons. I'd rather be with honest people who don't lie for months at a time to me. Even if it is your job," I said, my voice cracking, hoarse from yelling at the man I loved. Before I could stop myself, I was crying and looking out the window.

Though they also lived in Miami, their neighborhood was far away from Gianni's slick bachelor pad near South Beach. What the fuck had I been thinking? I was flying back and forth, sometimes for just one date and a few unforgettable hours in bed. My guard was down with him, and he'd waltzed right in, sensitive, sweet, masculine, and seemingly genuine in his attraction toward me.

Was this about the four hundred thousand dollars Concepcion left me? Or was there something else that would make me useful? If this investigation was about the money, I still had it. I'd placed it in a certificate of deposit at Canton State Bank. I hadn't thought much about it. Okay, that was a lie, every time I went shopping and saw something I really, desperately needed, like a new pair of T-strapped heels, I thought about getting it out and splurging on material items. But I didn't. Maybe I could just give it back. It seemed like I'd profited from my own misery. Money couldn't make anyone happy, including me.

Chapter Thirteen

Chantrea graciously let me in around eleven thirty p.m. She looked past me at Gianni's car and then shut the door.

"I don't know why you're here, but I am glad you came when you needed us. Let's get you to your room." She must have noting concern in my face. "Where did you get those shoes? I will have to borrow them."

She was polite not to insist I tell her what brought me to her doorstep, my stiletto shoes in my hand and my mascara coming undone at the corners of my eyes.

I couldn't relax completely after the night I had, but at least I could collapse into the guest bedroom and try to sleep away this nightmare. While I washed off my makeup in the bathroom, I heard Chantrea come downstairs.

"Good night, Joelle," she whispered before leaving. "We can talk about everything in the morning."

She left me some pajamas, a new T-shirt with the monogram "Disney World's Animal Kingdom" and a picture of the Tree of Life. That made me smile thinking of them at Disney World.

True kindness was in her voice. I hadn't been told anything really, but I did know my heart was breaking, and my stomach was in knots.

By the time I fell into a fitful sleep, I had already spent an hour on the phone with my little sister. I trusted her more than anyone else in my family, and I needed to vent before I could consider what to do. I left out some major details like I'd thought Gianni was going to propose. The thing about us McCoy girls was we rarely had our hearts broken because we didn't open them up to just anyone.

Our mother had made sure we watched enough talk shows when we were homesick that we were ready for all the shock and awe revelations anyone could come up with. Montel Williams and Maury Povich had educated us, well. And until now, I had successfully dodged many cheaters and liars from stealing my heart. I loved a man who lied to me, and I was pretty sure my former battle buddy had armed him with enough information to be my dream guy.

LaLa's advice was to hear him out, but, as soon as the truth was revealed, to gauge the level of the trail and then call her back. She needed more details before she could decide, just like her older sister.

"Joelle, it is not always what you think. Remember Grandma always says don't believe everything you hear and only half of what you see."

She did say that—a lot. I honestly didn't know if it ever meant anything to me then, but it might resonate for me now.

After finishing a couple of Asian pears Chantrea sliced up for me for breakfast, I waited in the living room for Gianni to pick me up. The usually very frank woman had not asked about the previous night's intrusion, and I did not offer an explanation. Whatever she assumed was the reason I came here last night was better than a lie I could come up with or, worse, the truth.

I hoped Gianni squirmed, thinking of me being out of his grasp, out of his bed. When his vehicle pulled into the driveway, I spared Chantrea from having to answer the door and ran outside.

I shut the door and walked toward the vehicle. Gianni waved like he was some teenage boy picking me up for a date. He looked anxious, nervous even.

"I'm glad to see you decided to come with me today."

"What choice do I have? I need answers, and you have none, so take me to where they are," I responded matter-of-factly, bitch mode turned on, ready for action.

He pulled away, and we eventually eased onto the highway, headed toward downtown. We rode in silence. I hated the way the air felt thick with emotion, but neither of us wanted to make the first move. When he turned to park near his office building, I was confused but somewhat relieved. If he had taken me to his condo, I would have had to see the remnants of our life together.

For two months I had lived with him and had made myself quite comfortable. It seemed silly now, but I considered what was mine was his, and what was his was mine. Good thing I got clued in. Only months of my life were wasted.

The offices were mostly closed for the weekend, but there was still a security guard posted to check purses. We took the stairs up to the office, and I was thankful I had decided on a casual outfit. I had left a few things at Chantrea's house on a previous visit, and one of them was a pair of tennis shoes. I couldn't fit them in my suitcase, and after many minutes, I had surrendered the shoes. Chantrea said she'd save them for my next trip to Florida.

Valderron was sitting in the small conference room at the FBI office. The secretary was off for the day, and this disappointed me. It would be nice not to be completely alone with these two.

"Is this it? Or is someone else joining us?" I demanded. Once I realized it only involved them, I wasn't going to be polite.

"Are you expecting someone else?" Valderron said, his gaze settling on me at last. There was a determination in his eyes I hadn't seen before. "To answer your question, we are not."

"Before you two get into why we're here, how come you haven't returned my calls?" I asked Valderron. Gianni seemed surprised to discover I was calling his partner.

"I didn't have any information until yesterday." He then clapped his hands loudly. "Let's get down to why we're here. You can deal with your issues later," Valderron continued with an authority in his voice I admired. I could see more of the reasons Concepcion fell in love with him. "We think Concepcion is still alive, and we want you to help us find her."

Valderron took in a deep breath after his announcement. I shifted in my seat. Yes, he did get down to business. I couldn't look directly at either of them. I wanted to cry from the sheer exhaustion of the moment. I had entertained the idea, but I needed more proof.

"Gianni, I want to hear from you," I said.

He contemplated whatever he was going to say a little too long for my temper.

"Now tell me everything you have been lying to me about since we met. What the fuck is going on?" My tears started to flow because of the anger boiling underneath my skin. His eyes met mine. I searched his face for the man I fell in love with. I could search all day and all night and still might not know the truth.

"Calm down, please, because this doesn't get any easier when you're shouting. You think I don't know what this means for us, having to keep this from you," Gianni said.

I couldn't look at him again. I did not want to see him explain. Valderron was on the edge of his seat and shifted some papers in a file I had not noticed before. He brought a paper from the back and put it on top of the pile.

"This is still news to me. Valderron had the information, but he wasn't sure what it all meant," he said. "I even told you some of it the first day I met you, simply because I had to see your reaction. We hadn't heard a peep from you in six months. Hell, we still don't know what it all means, but at this point, we had to bring you into this."

"Okay, why do you think she is alive? Let's see some evidence," I said, speaking like the journalist I was. Evidence, because that was the only thing that I trusted at this point. It sure as hell was not them.

Valderron handed me the file, the one he seemed to be considering since I got here. It looked worn out from use, and inside was what appeared to be a medical form with information about the cause of death for one Concepcion Ana Rael Chapa.

As I scanned the form, I found something that gave me a sense of hope and sadness at the same time. Whoever had died was pregnant at the time of death. It was this detail largely that made me consider the possibility that my friend could be walking around instead of being a pile of ash decorating the mantel of her parents' home. After a couple of years of friendship, my friend had shared with me a secret not found in any file the military had on her.

She'd had her Fallopian tubes tied when she came of age, out of the guilt and sadness associated with her abortions as a teenager. She'd explained this choice would be with her just like the choices she had made to end the lives of her unborn children. If she wasn't ready to be a mom at fourteen or sixteen years old, she didn't get to keep trying when she was older. Out of everyone I have ever met, Concepcion was harder on herself than anyone else could have ever been.

"Why would you make such a permanent decision at age twenty-two?" I had asked during one of our heart-to-hearts.

"And you don't think when I ended two pregnancies that it wasn't permanent? It was final. I permanently decided not to be a mom. I was not going to give myself a chance later."

Out of fear of a paper trail, Concepcion had gone to Mexico for the procedure. I suspected no doctor would agree to it in the United States since Concepcion had never been a mom.

This bit of information made me take a good look around at the two men who'd brought me into this room. If they knew this information, they would have told me. Surely Valderron and Concepcion had spoken about children or kids since they were together.

"Valderron, was this your child?" I asked, trying to gauge his reaction. "Is this why you are out there searching for answers?"

"She told me not to worry about birth control, and I honestly never did. If she had gotten pregnant to try to trap me into a marriage like my mama said all women would, I wouldn't have cared, that's how much I loved her. I would have loved to be the father of her child."

I believed him and felt a stab of guilt for being so callous about his feelings in all of this. He was missing her, too, and I was being insensitive. I decided to save my anger for Gianni.

Despite the guilt, I wasn't telling them anything until I'd heard everything. They'd certainly taken their sweet time bringing me in on this.

The rest of the file included bank information, all of which was suspect. I didn't know much about investigating, but the highlighted transfers didn't make it hard to connect the dots. There were large transfers of money before her death, but we couldn't quite figure out where it all ended up.

"Do you understand any of this, Joelle?" Gianni stood up from the table.

While I was scanning the pages in the file, his hand rested on my shoulder. The feeling of his being close to me once again brought up a few different responses. The light hairs on my arms stood at attention. His body was electric, but he was still cold to me. He was a damn good actor. I had to resist any physical contact from him.

"I need to focus on this for now." I buried my nose in the file. It was a gesture he understood.

Gianni withdrew his hand and sat back down beside me.

The next thing I felt was Valderron patting my shoulder as he left the room with his cell phone. I didn't blame him because he had been so close to Concepcion, close enough to one day marry her, and I was sure any man worth his salt would fight for the woman he loved. Even if it meant misleading her best friend. Gianni, on the other hand, did not get any of my sympathy.

"I think…" I started to say and paused. What did I think? "I think it is all suspicious but not concrete. Who identified this supposed body?"

"We also thought about that, but it was our boss, Aquila. He was as scrupulous as he should be. He is our superior, but no one is above suspicion. Not even you."

I breathed a heavy sigh. There was a reason Gianni had come to me, and it wasn't because I was a great salsa dancer. I had played right into his hands.

"I understood that soon after you started stuttering and mumbling last night. Do you think I was born yesterday? Or am I just some dumb hillbilly you can toy with? She was my best friend, you asshole. We knew each other long before she met you."

"Exactly," Gianni said, his tone agreeing with me. "We have to think about where she would go, who she would trust. I mean, for six months you had no contact with her family, and you had to be practically forced to collect the life insurance money. It sure as hell was suspicious."

I had been in disbelief when I heard the news. I had taken a call from a man halfway around the world. I had asked my grandma, and she found nothing. Someone had attached her name to a body already buried as a Jane Doe. This had only assured me that the death was faked.

The last thing I cared about was a friend's death benefits. Concepcion's money. I didn't think she would have ever left me something like that. She had a whole new life after the Army. She was in her own world. A world I didn't know enough about. I didn't know what my friend was up to before her supposed death. Or maybe she was dead, and this guy was still messing with my head. He could have some ulterior motive, like the money Concepcion left to me. People had killed for less, and Gianni admitted to meeting with suspicious intentions: he wanted to investigate me.

"Make this whole thing go so much smoother, and help us out. It has taken a long time to convince Valderron to trust you. He thought it was because of what we got going on together. I know you're hurting, but if there is a chance…" Gianni paused, pleaded. "A chance—"

"I'm here, aren't I? That's as much as I can say right now," I answered. "I am here."

I stared into his eyes. They seemed sad and different from before, cradled in weary bags. He hadn't slept all night, had he? How had he kept all this from me? It wasn't supposed to get complicated. I was sure whatever it was that brought us together was dying a slow death as all the facts emerged. Would he use me to find her? How far would he go?

It seemed I would have to go even further for the truth.

Valderron came back into the room but kept his phone on the table. He must be expecting a return phone call.

"Joelle, I haven't even told all of this to Gianni, but I want you to hear more about that postcard you found."

"What about it? Did you find any information about Clara and Carlos?" This question had been nagging at me since I had found the postcard in the book.

"I wasn't sure until yesterday, but it confirmed something that can't be explained," he said. The weary young man looked as if he was carefully weighing each word. "I genuinely believe you don't know what you found, which gives you more credibility than I originally thought. Clara and Carlos are code names for two former CIA agents who have close ties to four persons known to all of us."

"Who would that be?"

"First, our boss, Agent Aquila. And Jimm and Chantrea Mao, Chapa's adopted parents," he said. "That would make Clara and Carlos Concepcion's biological parents. They were active with the agency in the seventies with the Maos. Concepcion Chapa was their only child, born in 1982. By that point, they were out."

"I knew they worked in the government from Chantrea. She never told me they were in the CIA," I said, as shocked as Gianni looked. "So what are their real names?"

"How did you find the link to Aquila?" Gianni asked. "That's blowing my mind. Our boss having links to Concepcion's parents."

"Did Concepcion know her parents were agents or that Aquila worked with them?"

"She never told me anything about it, but I find it hard to believe she didn't know," Valderron said. "The funny thing is, it was literally right in front of our faces, Gianni. It's that photograph hanging in Aquila's office with all the badasses wearing sunglasses. The one where they're all standing in some South American jungle. Look at this."

Valderron set down a photocopy of the picture presumably hanging in Aquila's office. He was right. Her mom was smaller than Concepcion in the hips, with a Farah Fawcett haircut and aviator sunglasses. Her dad held his wife at the waist and another man around the neck. There were another blonde woman and two white guys in the photograph. They looked like a team, but I couldn't take my eyes off the three of them.

"Is this Aquila?" I pointed to the man next to Mr. Chapa.

"Good guess," Gianni said and smiled the first smile I had seen in a while. "This *cabron* is nearly fifty now, but he still looks like this so you would recognize him."

"What does this mean for Concepcion?" I asked. "It's a link to her parents, but not to her."

"I don't know. Sometimes I think Concepcion had to know about him. They looked like brothers in this picture. How did she end up under his command of all the people in the bureau?"

I was supposed to be her best friend, but there was still so much I never asked. I didn't bring up her parents often because it wasn't my place. If my parents died, would I want to keep answering questions about them? When Chapa told me she was legally adopted, at the time I didn't understand who she considered her parents. I now understood it was Carlos and Clara.

"Her mother was a professor of sociology and her dad sold home security systems," Valderron said. "I found out about the CIA work after I called a friend from Quantico."

"Is there any more that you guys want to tell me?" I asked, considering my next move.

"Not right now, what about you, Chuey?" Gianni asked Valderron. He then turned to me. "Will you stay and help us, Joelle? Will you come back and stay with me?"

"Maybe, but to answer your second question, not right now," I said, repeating the vague answer he just gave me. "I want to meet Aquila. I think I should be the one to ask some of our questions. What can he do to me? I'm not under his control, and since I'm not due back to my job any time soon, I can at least stay a couple of weeks. When can I meet him?"

"He gets back next Friday from Washington," Valderron said. He nodded and seemed to agree with me asking the questions. "I can send him an email that you asked to meet him and talk about Concepcion. It's harmless enough; you originally wanted to meet him, so I think the story will fly."

"Until then, I'm going home to get some rest,"

"Seriously, Joelle, you can stay with me. I won't

try anything," Gianni said. "I think we should just try to work through this together."

Valderron left the room. Good move. I was going to go hard on Gianni for what he did to me.

"Stay with you? You kept information from me when we were supposed to be building trust. A relationship kind of needs that." I closed my eyes and contracted my abdominals to try to physically restrain myself from crying and turning into the mess that he made me. I was wrong on so many levels to believe this was my future life partner. He made me want something I'd never allowed myself to think was real, an enduring romantic relationship built on good sex, mutual understanding, and intelligent conversations.

"I'll stay with you over my actual dead body."

Chapter Fourteen

It might have seemed like a waste of money to fly home for only a few days, but money was no object when it came to my sanity. Besides, I had plenty of money and staying one more minute with what I would call the ultimate buddyfuckers wasn't going to happen.

The term *buddyfucker* harkened back to good old basic training at Fort Jackson, South Carolina. The drill sergeant explained to my platoon that Private Wittier had just complained about the comfort, or lack thereof, of the twin mattresses we all slept on in the barracks. It was then we realized, we, all thirty-two of us, had been buddyfucked. That night, we were all punished equally because of one soldier's transgression, his complaints.

The term seemed to fit Valderron, Gianni, and, if she was alive, Concepcion herself. All said parties, at the very least, had lied to me; Gianni had used me. It had been truly my own naïveté and sex-deprived self who crawled into bed with one of the culprits, and I knew my future romantic relationships were fucked along with everything else. I really had some issues now. I didn't even have to make them up.

My going home was not a particularly welcome idea for those two, especially after the secret-file intervention with me. I pointed out that, first, I did what I wanted, and second, if they didn't trust me enough to go home, then my help wasn't necessary anyway. I left without their permission, but in my heart, I knew I would go back to Miami to find my own answers. I deserved to hear the truth.

Upon arriving at the St. Louis airport, I breathed a huge sigh of relief. It might not have the atmosphere of Miami, but my home was my refuge.

At the baggage claim, I watched as LaLa ran up to me and hugged me, I think more out of habit. Airport reunions were always good for some dramatic sisterly affection. At least I could rely on my own sister to give me a good hug.

"So, here she is…Miss America," she sang into my ear as she hugged me. She wasn't in uniform, but she flashed her badge, and we got through without having to pay for parking. I wished my military ID came with all those perks. All I got was a free dinner at Applebee's on Veteran's Day. I hated Applebee's.

"I need to regroup for at least a night," I announced in the car before she could guilt-trip me into going to my mom's house on the way.

I needed my own bed and my own things. On the hour-long ride to my rural home, LaLa filled me in on the latest happenings with the family. It was cathartic to hear about the divorce of a younger cousin who regarded my usually single status with contempt. It was the sixth marriage of my uncle who decided that getting hitched was a lot easier than dating long-term that finally made me laugh out loud while LaLa told me the story.

"You're laughing way too hard at someone who is blood-related, Joelle." LaLa grinned. "It might be hereditary to be this bad at love. I mean, look at our track record."

Touché'

As we drove on the winding hills into Marion County, the past year's events seemed like a bad dream. I hoped it couldn't get any worse. My latest trip to Miami was nothing like I thought it would be. I was manipulated by sunshine and a shady lover. If it were up to me, I would rather face guard duty in Iraq than be lied to by this man.

"Joelle, Joelle. Are you even listening to me?" LaLa lit a cigarette and rolled down her window part of the way. I hated her smoking, so to punish her, I rolled my window down all the way, so it was impossible to hear anything but the wind. I heard her mutter something about me acting like a bitch, but it just took one of her cigarettes in her car, and I was pissed off at her again, too.

After what seemed like the longest cigarette break ever, she finally finished, and we closed the windows.

"Don't give me that look," she said.

I wasn't giving her any kind of look, but it was habit to be upset by her making bad choices. She was a police officer; how much more dangerous did she have to make her life?

"Did you read the book I gave you about addictions?" I had sent it from Miami, and all the reviews seemed positive. In my opinion, it was who she surrounded herself with who posed all the problems, including my mom, who was a chain-smoker from way back. If Mom lit up, LaLa would soon follow, and it had been that way since LaLa was seventeen years old.

"If you are not coming to the house, then we are coming to you. I need to be with my sister. I want to help," LaLa declared.

I knew that my family just wanted to pry into my business; it was our way of doing things. I was guilty of it as well. I wouldn't be able to handle it. Not after the past few days I had.

It didn't matter what I said about wanting to be alone, my family came anyway. My dad was the only smart one who stayed home. My mom brought over some famous rotisserie chicken jambalaya, and I watched my older sister, Emma, feed small pieces of roasted red peppers and chicken to my one-year-old niece. She was too cute, and I caught myself smiling at her despite my bad mood. She offered me a piece of her mishmash of food in her tiny chubby fist.

"Yum, yum," she nodded.

I took it from her, and despite my bratty mood, I ate and smiled.

"Yum, yum. You're right."

Zoey's four-year-old sister, Chelsea, was already finished eating and making faces at me from across the table. They sure knew how to cheer me up.

Later that evening, after they left and LaLa helped me unpack some boxes, I climbed into my bed with fresh sheets and cried for the tenth time since Gianni had pulled the car over and ruined my life.

I let it out. At home, I could moan and scream, and snot could drip onto my pillow. No one here could judge me or my sadness. Tonight was the last night I would cry over Gianni. Easier said than done, but I said it out loud to make it more official.

Tomorrow, I had work to do. Concepcion Chapa was a person I thought I knew better. Someone had brought me into this mess, and it would take some serious work to get myself out. I contemplated telling LaLa about everything because she might be able to assist with some background information on Gianni, Valderron, and this Aquila guy. LaLa had contacts. On the other hand, she was a civil servant and would have more at stake because of the badge. Deciding to involve her was a last resort.

I caressed my legs underneath the sheets lightly, just as he would have done. I felt the smoothness of my skin and my muscled thighs. It just wasn't the same.

To change my train of thought from Gianni, I closed my eyes and tried to visualize Concepcion's face. I searched what was left in my memory for any indication of why this was happening. But her smile didn't budge, and I could almost hear her voice.

I still had a little film we had made saved on my laptop along with thousands of photographs from various places we had found ourselves throughout the years. It was not the same. Her deep brown eyes and chin-length hair came to represent her to me now, though I had seen her wear it a million different ways.

Our conversations had been few and far between before her alleged death. It still bothered me that I was either too selfish or too jealous to be a better friend, one who visited. In truth, I had been envious that she was living an even more exciting life in Miami than we had experienced together. I had just gone back to the beginning, back to the comfortable town, the security of a part-time job and my new farmhouse.

The truth was, I could have followed her to Miami and added FBI agent to my résumé. I was bitter about my time in the military and a little jealous of her success. Back home, I was somebody; I was important. But in Miami, I would have had to earn it. I would have had to push through another man's world, and the Army had been plenty for one lifetime. When it all came down to it, I wasn't ready to follow her on another adventure.

My heart fluttered when I saw Gianni at the Miami Airport, but when he tried to kiss my lips, I pulled away and dragged my suitcase behind me. He was taking it hard, I could tell. He looked like he hadn't slept the whole time I was gone, but it wasn't my fault he couldn't trust me with the truth. He'd explained to me in a midnight phone call that it had started as a way to get information, but he fell in love with me despite the case. I understood it; I just couldn't put away the idea of him investigating me from the very beginning. I wasn't mad anymore; I was just done. We had started something, and he had finished it by not being honest with me. It didn't matter that my heart was pounding when he was close to me. Pound away. I wasn't going to let him hurt me again, not when so much was at stake with finding my best friend.

Once we were in the car, Gianni asked, "Where to?"

"Please take me to Chantrea and Jimm's house," I said. "They are expecting me. I even brought her a photo book of farm scenes from the airport in Missouri."

I asked myself why I was talking to him, but no matter how angry I was, it didn't seem possible to ride the forty-five minutes to their house in silence.

"That's nice of you. Chantrea must be happy to have you around. It seems like you two hit it off."

"Yeah, I think I will keep visiting her and Jimm. I have the money, and she is a genuine person. She also cooks the most amazing food I've never heard of."

"She sure does. Concepcion and I stopped by their house quite a bit to get lunch back in the day. She always had something spicy for us to burn our mouths with, and that's saying something from a Sicilian in Miami. We know spicy."

His last comment gave me a tingling feeling, an amorous one. I tried to hide my bitterness and stay focused. Gianni was attractive to the point of distraction, and his casual clothes for the airport pickup were not too shabby. He was wearing those same jeans he'd worn to the beach but with a gray tight-fitted V-neck T-shirt that showed off a hint of his tanned chest. He probably planned it that way.

Despite the tension, we were carrying on a conversation like a couple of adults. At a stoplight, Gianni reached his hand over and set it on my bare leg. I was wearing a denim skirt, not a mini, but enough to make him pause when he saw me.

"Not now, Gianni," I considered his searching eyes. "I'm not ready for any of that. I came here to focus on getting answers, but then I will leave."

"And what if you don't find the answers, will you stay?"

It was a fair question, but I didn't answer. I thought it was enough to refuse his kiss and move his hand for him to understand I wasn't sure about anything anymore.

"What's your favorite thing Chantrea makes?" I wanted to break the silence. "I want to tell her when I get there."

"I don't know what it's called, but it's a cold salad with papaya, fish sauce, and lime juice," he said. "She mixed in peppers from her garden that made me cry, but I kept eating it."

"I know what you mean, she puts fish sauce in everything, and it tastes so much better," I said. It was true, and I'd found myself searching for fish sauce after my first trip to Miami. To no avail, we didn't have it in Canton. I had forgotten to ask LaLa to check in the St. Louis Asian food stores.

My mind went through the many scenarios of Gianni genuinely caring for me or using me for information. In a web I had yet to untangle, one where I was surrounded by people who were lying or at the very least withholding information, I decided I had to keep a firm grip on reality. Gianni and Valderron's campaign of misinformation was similar to the Army's use of psychological warfare. I wasn't going to be caught off guard with these two.

It was the morning I would meet Aquila, and my

stomach was not cooperating. I wasn't sure if it was nerves or the sushi I had eaten the night before, but I was worried. Even after going over and over the questions with Gianni and Agent Valderron, I couldn't shake the feeling that it was a do-or-die moment.

I came into the office and exchanged greetings with Luanne and the guys. I didn't want to seem too chummy with everyone, but Aquila was bound to know we would be friends. While I waited for Aquila to get off the phone and invite me in, I quickly checked the notepaper in my purse with my list of questions. I tried to create a mental note of everything on my list.

The most important question, among several throwaways, was how he knew it was Concepcion?

Just as I was second-guessing my Old Navy sundress and denim jacket, a very handsome, older man came into view.

"You must be Joelle," Aquila said. We shook hands and went into his office, where I swallowed hard at all the leather surrounding me. Damn that eel roll. He smelled of cigars, and I guessed the habit would fit in nicely with the machismo decorating style.

"Thank you for meeting with me, sir," I said as I sat in the oversized office chair. "I know we missed each other, what was it, three months ago, but I still have a few things I wanted to find out."

"I bet you do," he said. "She was your best friend, wasn't she? I wouldn't put the two of you together in a room."

His comment caught me off guard. "Oh, really, why's that?"

"You're just two different kinds of women, that's all," he said. "If you don't mind me saying so, it's hard to picture you in a uniform."

I did mind him saying so, but I had to stay focused on what we were doing here. I was the last line of defense. Gianni and Valderron had no easy way to ask these questions and keep their jobs.

"Thank you, sir." I stared him dead in the eye. I might not be as tough as Concepcion, but I was no doe-eyed girl who took any compliment handed out to her.

"Drop the 'sir,' sweetheart, we're not in the goddamn Army. I suppose you're here because you think your friend is alive, not dead."

This conversation wasn't going anything like I planned. I was pretty sure he had the upper hand, and I wasn't sure how I should phrase my response.

"Yes, I am here to ask about that. Apparently, she just disappeared one day and was mistaken as a Jane Doe and buried without the fanfare of a decorated veteran."

"That's right, and it's a damn shame," he replied.

His smug grin was no longer visible; as I stared longer, I thought I saw a tear. "She was the best, wasn't she?"

I leaned forward in the too-comfortable leather chair. "She really was…" I paused and then decided now was as good a time as any. "Were you two close?"

"You could say that," he said. "We were like a sort of family in a way. I knew her real parents very well."

His honesty caught me off guard. It was unexpected. Valderron and Gianni had given me a very different idea about who this man was.

"Well, I didn't know them, and I'm sorry to say I didn't ask Concepcion what they were like,"

He pointed at a photo on the wall, which I already knew well.

"We met a long time ago, back when Miami was a much different town," he said. "I'm Cuban, and her parents were Puerto Rican, so naturally we had some differences, but we made one hell of a team. Did Concepcion tell you her mama was an expert marksman? I mean, she was the best."

These were not things that Chapa shared with me. My skin burned hot with jealousy when I resolved there was a legacy of government service that my best friend had never revealed to me. With so much time invested in our friendship, I realized I was the only open book between the two of us.

After an hour, my legs were going to sleep, but I didn't want to interrupt. I barely got in an "oh, wow" or a "why's that?"

I wondered if the guys were pressed up against the door. I wondered if they had the same effect on their boss. I was a journalist. It didn't take any special skill to get him to speak about Concepcion. He was as ready for this conversation as me.

"That's the saddest part, though, their own daughter was the last of them," he said. "She was pregnant, you know."

I tried to look surprised. I thought he was buying it. How could I know she was pregnant? I was just the ole battle buddy coming back to meet her team.

"I didn't know that. Valderron didn't mention it." I tried to sound shocked.

"She told me, but she hadn't told him yet," he said. "She confided in me right before she died. Even though I'm just an old man, she trusted me. She told me about some operation in Mexico that she regretted, but apparently, it hadn't stuck, because there she was pregnant. She treated me like a kind of uncle. I was happy to be there for her, and I'm still sad there is nothing left from that family worth going on about. Warriors, they were, every one of them. I remember Clara pregnant, and I wanted that happiness for

Concepcion."

"Have you told Agent Valderron about the baby?" I asked. "I would want to know if I were him."

"Am I the right person to bring it up to him? He has a copy of the report; he knows," he nodded. "It's not like that here anymore. With Concepcion gone, our team isn't the same, and I'm too old to be anyone's babysitter. I hurt, too, goddammit. It's like they didn't even know her."

"Were you secretive about your relationship with her?" I asked. "Or about the fact that she was like family?"

"Of course I was; otherwise they never would have let me be her supervisor. The bureau is funny like that, but that's like the military. I would show her special treatment or something; she didn't need kid gloves or handholding because she was just that good. Fuck the bureau and its rules."

He turned to me with tears in his eyes; he seemed genuine. How had Gianni and Valderron been so wrong? All I saw was a man in pain, just like they were, just as I was, but I was healing, and we might as well heal together.

"Thank you, sir, I mean, Special Agent Aquila." I stood up to shake his hand. "I got what I came here for, and it was a pleasure hearing about Concepcion again from someone who knew her well."

"You're welcome, Miss McCoy. I'll see you out."

"That's okay. I think I'll stop by and say goodbye to the guys."

"As you wish." He wiped his eyes. I extended my hand but then decided against it. He hugged me first, and I hugged him right back, hard. I nodded slowly to myself, with a sense of relief.

It was only a few hours later, and I was already packing my clothes at Chantrea and Jimm's house. Gianni and Valderron were off doing what they did best, which was digging for evidence to support the answers from Aquila. They wanted verification and vindication, and I didn't blame them. I just wasn't going any further with it because I really didn't think that was what Concepcion would have wanted. I was awake to the fact that her disappearance was clouding my senses; Aquila had given me closure. There was just too much personal information that couldn't be faked. I knew he knew her.

Chantrea knocked lightly, and then I heard her enter through the partially closed door.

"Leaving so soon?" she said. "Or are you going to stay with your friend?" My *friend*. Chantrea sure knew how to be tactful about Gianni.

"I'm going to catch the red-eye back to St. Louis. Don't worry, though, I'm planning on coming back real soon." I gingerly patted her shoulder. "You and Jimm will always have a future guest in me. You made me love this city and your cooking."

"I guess that's true," she said. "You had a good appetite tonight; you ate like I've never seen you."

I was going to miss having all her food at my fingertips.

"We need to have you open a restaurant in Canton. I would eat whatever you served up."

"Oh, no. I just want to serve my friends and family. Thank you," she said. "I haven't been able to show it off to anyone but Jimm, and he has been eating it for thirty-five years."

"Is there anything you want or need, Chantrea?" I asked. "I still have all this money left, and I wondered if you had any ideas on what I should do with it."

"I can't believe that's true, a young girl like you not knowing how to spend her money? You and Concepcion are just alike. She asked a question like that years ago, asking me what I would do if I won the lottery or hit it big at the casinos Jimm and I go to."

"Well, what did you tell her?"

"I told her I wasn't really sure, that a life with all that money might be harder because earning money to live is what gets most people up out of bed every day," she said. "I don't know if that was the right thing to say, but she didn't ask again. She did buy something, though, after we talked, something I still have here somewhere."

She left the room, and after I heard her rummaging in a storage closet, she came out with an expensive-looking globe, still spinning from her touch.

I took it from her outstretched hand and set it on the bed.

"Show me the places you have visited, Joelle. I'm curious to see between the two of us what ground we have covered."

I pointed to much of the Middle East, El Salvador, Mexico, Canada, Germany, and the Caribbean. After my turn, Chantrea patiently showed me most of Southeast Asia and China, Australia, New Zealand, most of Europe, Madagascar, and even Cuba, where she had gone as an academic speaker for the University of Miami.

"Wow, you've got me beat," I shrugged. "Any place you think I should visit?"

"Go somewhere I've never been and try to make a difference in whatever way you can. It's not the places you go, but the people you meet. Make new friends and start smiling again. She would want that for you."

"Sounds like fun, Chantrea. If I go anywhere, you'll be the first one I write to."

"Oh, I hope not." She laughed. "Drop a line to that Gianni friend of yours, he looks like a nice traveling partner. And he likes spicy food, too, that counts for something."

Chapter Fifteen

October 6, 2010

In an internet café near the capital city of Kosovo, my life turned upside down once again. It was because of her. I clicked on an email from an address that included my first and last name in the subject line. It had gone straight to my junk mail automatically but so did a lot of important emails. The simple message read like a threat. The words written on the page gave me an instant stomach ache.

"You lost my two friends, and now you are getting warmer. And that's not a safe thing to do. Go home,

McCoy."

I logged out by instinct, by fear. I looked around at the other people checking Facebook, surfing YouTube, and downloading music. No one seemed interested in me. The email rattled me to the core. I reconsidered what that meant. The only person who called me McCoy instead of Joelle was Concepcion. That meant there was a real possibility Concepcion was alive.

We both had different lives now, and mine was just getting started. My adventures were only just beginning, the ones without her by my side.

It was a thrill living halfway across the world to volunteer my time with a nongovernmental organization. I was helping others, but mostly, I was helping myself move on. These past few months were a new chapter in my life.

I started freelancing for the Associated Press whenever I could write about something that would sell back home. My audience was mostly the Americans who couldn't find Kosovo on a map but still remembered that we bombed Serbia on behalf of the Kosovo-Albanians. I did get some worldwide coverage when I mentioned the NATO forces while we still had troops there in minuscule amounts. The stories about black-market deals and underage-girl trafficking from neighboring Balkan states insured I had a byline and a paycheck. Real shock and awe kind of stories. I wrote a couple of human-interest pieces for the local paper in Missouri. I could always hang my hat on community journalism. They were mostly about food, including recipes and cute photos of shop windows and wrinkled grandmothers with headscarves.

Since Kosovo declared independence in 2007, many of the peacekeeping soldiers from the NATO mission were pared down. With the international presence, a lot of money was pumped into the local economies for job creation and stability. There was a sense of new normalcy. The capital city had a shopping mall like everywhere else in the modern world. Next step, a McDonald's.

I wasn't here with the military, but it was nice to see some familiar uniforms in the capital, Pristina. For many reasons, the mission in Kosovo was a positive thing, and most of the population seemed to be happy NATO forces were there.

I paid for my macchiato and left a tip at the internet café I had spent the last two hours in, mostly thinking. It was still early in the afternoon but only seven a.m. in Missouri. My first thought was to call Gianni so he could help me figure out what to do about the email. Valderron and Gianni were correct in their suspicions, but they had used me for information on Chapa and waited way too long to tell me about the possibility. That meant Aquila lied, too. He had seemed convincing, and I asked myself what that meant. He seemed to know the most about her beside me, but he was also the one who stopped my search.

I walked the two city blocks to the apartment which I shared with two other women.

Entering through the front door, I smelled comfort food in Kosovo. Comfort food meant a hearty meat pocket called *borek*. One of my roommates was a Kosovo-Albanian with US citizenship. She was in Kosovo conducting research for her doctorate in international relations. She came back with her boyfriend, Fatim, who was doing the same thing in Macedonia.

"Something smells good," I hollered into the kitchen area. "Make enough for me?"

Hida called back as I changed from boots into my flip-flops. It was customary to remove shoes at the door, especially with my European roommates, who were much tidier than me. I had an excuse, though, which I used when they made fun of the way I did something; "I'm a dumb American" usually worked. Our apartment building neighbors represented a list of countries I'd never visited. We were all united in our neighborhood of furnished apartments with the fact that we were strangers in a strange land, mostly trying to do some good or earn a better paycheck.

"What's up? Have you been cooking all day like a housewife or something?" I asked Hida as we greeted each other with kisses on both cheeks. Her massive amount of straight dark hair was pulled back with a bandanna with the Albanian flag on it. Her light blue eyes examined me.

"There's enough for you if you didn't fill up on brioche at the café," she examined the powdered sugar still left on my black shirt.

Hida and I were spending a lot of our free time together, mainly because we both embraced the roommate experience. I had decided not to live alone while I stayed here because I wanted to meet other people. I had already called Chantrea and told her I could add several more countries to my list.

Kosovo was like Missouri in many ways. Rural, but hopeful, and most people smiled on the street, even at strangers. Technology made it easy to stay in touch with my family, and I emphasized how nice my roommates were and how it was like any other European city. I wasn't sure anyone liked the idea of me being away, but only my mom was honest enough to tell me to come back as soon as possible.

LaLa was worried because she kept up with the

news and read about the region's history. Living here was a different story than anyone could ever read about on the internet. Every morning a voice called most Muslims to prayer over the loudspeaker. The voice had a youthful quality to it and a ritualistic nature. I was reminded of my grandmother's rooster waking up the house, whether we liked it or not. It reminded me of Iraq, and it made me smile to think about what united us as people.

"We can eat this for lunch in a few minutes with the *borek*," Hida stirred a pot of something that smelled like vegetable beef soup.

"I'm starving. I'll be in my room; just call me when it's ready," I said with a pang of guilt for not helping.

Without Hida's cooking, I would have overdosed on Nutella and French bread. I walked along the dark hardwood floors and up the stairs to my room. The hardwood floors throughout the entire house were an extravagance in my mind, but the rent was reasonable enough.

I looked out my window into the bustling streets. This was an international neighborhood, and the streets were bare during the workdays. Besides the shop owners, it seemed the only people who had jobs here were foreigners. There was widespread corruption and a ruthless black market, but things were getting better, according to all the positive press Kosovo was receiving in the news. Hida spoke about the many things she would change if she had political power, and the one major issue we agreed on was making sure all children, regardless of their ethnicity, could get an education. In her opinion, an educated population would eventually fix itself. I agreed.

I stretched out on my twin bed and let my mind go back to the email. I should have printed it for proof, but who would I show it to? No one, it would be too risky. I wasn't trying to make waves here, and just as I was getting settled in my new surroundings, I got an email that opened the past for discussion. Did she mean I was just supposed to leave Pristina, Kosovo, or the whole of Europe? Somehow, I doubted I could send a reply. I would have to think about what that would mean for me.

I worked in Pristina with female domestic violence victims and their children. It wasn't called a shelter for community reasons, but we did provide a home, food, daycare, and schooling for the children. Our clients came in all shapes and sizes. Ethnicity was not a barrier. They escaped from broken families, torn apart by violence and then shunned by the entire community.

The leader of the shelter, Mina, kept me on my toes. She reminded me of Concepcion. One day I told her about my missing friend while we were unloading boxes.

"You are only missing one friend. I am missing at least a dozen of my classmates from school. The war took so many people to different parts of the world."

I reconsidered having any future pity parties with her.

The women we helped all had different stories like Mina, but helping them in my own small ways made me feel better. The reality of my military service never came close to the way I felt about working here.

About twenty women were staying on a permanent basis at the shelter. We had a capacity for twice that number, but throughout the few months I worked there, ten women and their children had left or graduated out and went on their own. *Would they make it out there?* I asked myself each time one of them left. I wanted to keep checking on them after they were gone, but that wasn't what we did.

External counseling was available through another sister organization, and as they packed up individually, I was reminded of when I left home for each new adventure. I was twenty-seven years old, and I had packed my share of duffel bags and suitcases. Mina ran her own type of boot camp for women, teaching them independence and self-awareness. No one could teach self-esteem, but we damn well tried to instill it. Above the door of the shelter, Mina had hung a hand-painted sign of a well-known Latin proverb. "*Venin, Vidi, Vici,*" or in English, "I came, I saw, I conquered." Julius Caesar would be proud.

Even more difficult than watching the women leave was watching the children go with them. The children made me think about my own nieces and how much these kids were like them.

Throughout my time at the shelter, I concluded that kids were kids, no matter where you were. I regretted not spending more time understanding that as a soldier. I loved being the fun helper who funneled candy to the kids even after their mother said enough. I countered the effects by teaching a course on oral hygiene. The hardest part of the class was trying to keep the kids from eating the toothpaste, which I knew from experience was a universal problem. I had helped teach a similar course as a soldier in Iraq. It was courses like hygiene and group exercise that were supposed to foster goodwill and trust with the women.

This time there was no uniform or weapons. Instead of lugging an M16 everywhere during the classes, I could feel less like a commando and more like an instructor. It was freer. The Kosovars were no strangers to NATO soldiers with weapons in general.

They were still patrolling the streets day and night in Pristina. The mood was completely different. Violence was not a daily, weekly, or even monthly event. I found myself thinking about what Iraq would look like in ten years. Would it be like Kosovo?

The longer I was here, the more I reflected on my time in Iraq. I found myself questioning if what I had done as a soldier had contributed to any greater good.

Was it worth it? Did I do anything that would last? I still didn't know the answer, and I accepted the fact I probably never would.

I had read about the women's home in a news article from the Missouri National Guard when it had over five hundred soldiers deployed as part of the NATO mission.

I looked up an affiliate agency and asked Mina, who was quoted in the article, how I could help. My original plan was to send money or supplies, but after many conversations with Mina, I wanted to do more. Mina explained the hardships I would have to be ready to face.

"What do you not like about Kosovo?" LaLa asked me on a call. "It seems like you are happier there than here."

For starters, the electricity went out every so often, but after the first couple of weeks, I got used to it, much in the same way we got used to tractors driving slow on the main roads or even raw meat hanging in the store shop windows. Still, it was different. Our landlord had several generators, and we were lucky to have a backup system.

Truthfully, it was nice to be in a place where it wasn't always go, go, go or work, work, work.

Any appointments made with our local vendors for the women's shelter were guaranteed to be a half an hour late if not more, simply because the other person had stopped for a chat at the coffee shop or had run an errand for their family. Time was relative. It had been a year and a half since I got that crazy phone call about Concepcion's death. I considered it another catalyst in my life.

For the first time since I received Concepcion's death benefit, I was happy to be using it. But if I was right in assuming the email was from Concepcion, then I wasn't sure how I felt about the money anymore.

A voice called out to me in the bedroom. It was Hida telling me dinner was ready.

I had to catch myself from tripping on the steps to make it to the kitchen. If I didn't walk near ten miles a day around the city, I would have put on twenty pounds by now with the way she cooked all the time. I appreciated the home-cooked meals. Comfort foods always reminded me of home.

Throughout the meal, which Hida insisted we eat at the table, our Finnish roommate, Maria, told us about her latest shopping trip at the mall in Pristina. There was large street art showing near the shopping center, made by local artists with supplies donated to a youth center.

"It's really incredible. The kids were spray painting graffiti on the streets and on the shop walls. It was a good day," Maria said. "My favorite was a Roma boy's artwork of a map of Kosovo. All the locations were separated by ethnicity, but Pristina looked like a rainbow. His cows were vibrant and beautiful. What a talent and he knew his geography better than me."

"I should go down there and take pictures," I spooned in Hida's creation. "Maybe I can get Mina to let some of us go as a group."

"You really should, and then come by the Finnish camp if you want," Maria replied. We ate our meal in contemplation.

Maria had been working as a massage therapist at the Swedish and Finnish camp on contract here for about a year. She came off to me as a free spirit and a healer. I took in numerous wellness tips from her.

I thanked Hida for the wonderful meal and insisted on cleaning up while she went for a run around the complex. I replayed the email message while washing the dishes. How was I getting close to Concepcion? I had been here for a few months and hadn't been anywhere else except for a short trip to Macedonia when I met Hida's boyfriend. He was crazy about Hida, and that was all I needed for my approval. Concepcion must be in the Balkans somewhere, but how could she have been tracking me? She must be working for the government in some capacity. I understood now that our government could make anything happen to anyone.

While I scrubbed the soup pot, the small radio we had in the kitchen played an endless German techno song. It was infectious, and I made unbelievable time finishing the dishes. I was happy here, and Concepcion would have to do a lot more than send me an email to get me to leave.

Later that night, Hida and I walked the downtown streets of Pristina near the Ambassador Hotel and one of the main UN buildings. We had been attending salsa lessons with a very sassy Argentinian instructor, who worked as a civilian police officer. She was one hell of a dancer and, during her free hours, taught us, mere mortals, the art of dance. If only Gianni could see me in the class. I loved what the workouts were doing for my body. It was sexy. It must have shown on my face because after class when Hida was chatting with our instructor, a younger guy came up and handed me his card. He was an Aussie and looked decent enough, but I gave him back his card and said, "I am with someone."

Later, Hida wanted to know who I considered myself with, and I couldn't answer her. I was with myself; wasn't that enough?

"I have had my fun in the last year, and I don't want to settle down with just anyone. I want an honest man who makes me feel like Gianni did, still does." I whispered the two last words, hoping Hida didn't hear my delusions.

I walked a little faster to distance myself from the building where other salsa students were congregating. I had confided in Hida about my man issues almost immediately upon arrival. It was a good sign when we became roommates that we could confide in each other so easily.

"Joelle, no man is perfect," she said. "And neither are we."

Our friendship was a first for her. Her large extended family made it easy to be isolated in ethnic Albanian culture. She dated other Albanians and worked for, and with, other Albanians. Her time in an American high school and college should have been an opportunity to expand her horizons, but the shock of a new country, language, a new everything meant Hida was less inclined to try anything else new. She was a Muslim, and in a post-nine-eleven world, she didn't share much with her other classmates. She told me on my second night in our apartment that I was her first real American friend and, strangely, we had met in Kosovo. It was a small world.

In theory, because she had American citizenship, she understood what it meant to be an American better than I did. On paper, we were the same, but our lives and backgrounds were very opposite from one another. In this, we were both good representations of an ever-changing definition of what it meant to be an American. Sister, daughter, soldier, friend, journalist, volunteer, these were all labels I identified with, but it took the experience of being surrounded by people from all over the world for me to fully embrace my country. No matter what I thought about the president or the politics, the first thing new people asked me was what country I was from, and in Kosovo, I was proud to be an American. Immigration was what our country was built on.

Later that night, I called LaLa. She was busy spending more time with my older sister, Emma, and our two nieces. I heard more about the girls and less about police work.

"I'm jealous, Joelle," she said. "You're living it up

and saving the world while I'm arresting old fogies for indecent exposure outside the mall. When are you coming home?"

I couldn't answer her question, so I talked around it. I relented after a few minutes of internal dialogue about whether to tell her about Concepcion or to keep my mouth shut. "Before I tell you something, I need you to know I can't be specific, and you can't tell anyone."

"Okay, of course," she said a little sarcastically. "I won't tell, but it had better be good. I have a feeling it is."

"I haven't decided if it's good for me or not, but here goes." I paused and thought about exactly how I should phrase it. How could I let her know this huge secret without making her worry, even just for a second? In all actuality, we didn't speak much about Concepcion anymore.

"I want you to take a second and think about the most important friend I have ever had, someone who has changed my life many times over." I stammered a bit but caught myself.

"Me, of course," LaLa laughed. "I am *the* most important friend you'll ever have, besides Emma."

"Not family, you shouldn't have to think long about this one," I said. "What if I said she may be alive."

LaLa didn't answer for a while.

After a few long silent minutes, I wasn't sure if she was even still on the line. I finally asked, "Are you still there?"

"I'm here," she said. "I know who you mean, but, honestly, I don't know what to think. What does this even mean for you? I thought you were moving on."

"I will never move on, not if there is hope," I said. "I really don't know."

"Is that what this is, hope?"

"No, it's much more than that. It's proof."

LaLa sighed. "Just be careful, please. If this person really is your friend, she'll understand."

Chapter Sixteen

After a particularly long day of work at the shelter, I decided to go against my instinct of falling asleep with my clothes on and call Gianni on a phone card instead of on Skype at the internet café. I wanted to be alone in a booth rather than out in the open with prying eyes, especially after Concepcion's email. It was getting easier to talk to Gianni after his betrayal; time was healing the wounds. He was a good conversationalist, and he actually picked up when I called, unlike many of my family members.

"To what do I owe the pleasure of your call?" he said after answering on the second ring. "And don't tell me another story about your roommate; I want to hear about you."

"No, well…" I hesitated. "Hida is involved, but I wanted to tell you we're taking salsa lessons from an Argentinian instructor. This lady is better than you."

"Oh, really, I doubt that; otherwise you wouldn't be calling to tell me," he said in a mocking yet flirty sort of way. "Actually, I'm not convinced you need the lessons."

"Are you kidding me? When we went out, I could barely get the correct rhythm. All I could do was shake my hips and let you lead me around."

"Exactly." He closed his speech, sounding satisfied with himself. There was a long pause, and I thought we lost the connection.

"Are you still there?" I asked.

"Yes, I'm here. I was just thinking, that's all."

"Well, don't. You know it's not your strong suit."

"Hey, what was that for?" he was defensive.

"No real reason," I joked, I wanted to push him just a little, play with him, wherever he was, Miami or not. I wasn't ever sure with his caseload. "I just wanted to hear your voice."

It became clear to me as we spoke that I had been missing him more than I let on. I couldn't be sure of what to do next. Not so long ago, I was thinking he would ask me to move in with him or even marry him.

The whole thing left a bitter taste in my mouth, mostly for my own naïveté.

We kept speaking about our work for at least another hour. He sounded like he needed to vent, and I let him. I really didn't have any problems to complain about, and I felt silly bringing up the everyday occurrences in a country he wouldn't understand. He did comment on how much better I sounded. Happier, I guessed he meant.

"I am happier, Gianni," I said. "Happier in a different way than at home. This is more about me than the women I get to help every day."

Eventually, he asked the inevitable question. "When do you think you'll come home?"

Home. I guessed he meant my farmhouse in Missouri, but I wasn't so sure anymore.

"I'm still working on that."

"Well, let me know. I can even come there to visit if you want."

I want; I want. Part of me, well, a lot of me, wanted to leave right away and go back to how everything was before I knew better. This time, though, my experience and its false promises held me back.

"Okay, I can let you know if I think that would work out."

We made plans to speak again later in the week. I

thought of him sitting in his home office in Miami, leaning back in the chair and contemplating our future like I was doing.

I hoped he realized this was a lot for me, to continue speaking to him after he stole my heart and made me doubt everything continuously. It wasn't enough to lose my best friend. I had to start over, knowing that I found a man I could truly love, and it was all based on investigating me. I was halfway around the world and could drop off the grid very easily. I wasn't sure I could hold in my feelings for him forever.

After I hung up, I decided to have a quick look at my email on one of the open computers.

I felt my stomach drop as I read the email from LaLa. It was short like Concepcion's email. What was up with short emails? She never wrote so little. The monitor flickered, and the power was out. Just like that, the email was erased from the screen.

"Fuck!" The expletive fell from my lips. I felt like a stranger here all at once. "Grandma's sick. I think you need to come home. Call me." It was signed, "love, LaLa." I contemplated using the phone, but the power and phone lines were out, and I couldn't wait. I ran out the door after paying for the phone call with Gianni.

Once at home, I dialed using our phone and my

calling card. LaLa answered on the second ring. It had been eight hours since she sent the news.

"How is she?"

"She's hanging in there, Jo, but honestly it's not looking good," she said over the hospital noise. The whole family must be together.

"Tell her to come home now," my mom said in the background.

The noise from the other end died down, and I figured my sister left the room. I was grateful because I needed to hear what was really going on without the whole family dictating my actions.

At some point I started to cry, a gut reaction to anything happening to my grandma.

"Are you outside now?" I asked her, trying to control my tears.

"I am, but I'm sure Mom is going to follow. It's crazy here. Grandma had a stroke, and they still don't know the extent of everything yet. Mom thinks if she just would have taken her sooner, it wouldn't be like this."

"Well, where was she when it happened?"

I kept praying silently that my phone card had enough minutes left. In my haste to hear my sister, I had bypassed the automatic option to check the card's balance.

"I guess she was lying down for a nap and didn't wake up. Grandpa was at the feed store, and two hours later, Mom came to pick her up for their hair appointments and—"

I heard a gasp and then the tears. We were both crying now.

"Jo, she has to come out of this. She's not even that old. She has never even gotten seriously sick or anything," she pleaded with me, as if I determined my grandmother's state. As if I could will her back to health. I tried to be there for my sister, who was dealing with the whole family without me.

"Grandma's tough as they come. Hell, if it had been her in Iraq, she would have been kicking asses and taking names. She is going to get through this," I said, trying to find strength in my own words. "She will, I promise. She's way too strong. Kiss and hug her for me."

I felt selfish for being away, even if it was only temporary. When something important happened, I wasn't there. I could already hear my mom swearing up and down because I wasn't there. It was also a big reason why she wanted me out of the military; she needed us to be close so she could run our lives, or at least attempt the task. Guilty, that was how I felt, just guilty.

After I hung up, my next call went to Mina's cell phone. She answered almost before it rang.

"Mina here." She said her name, no traditional telephone greetings for her. After I discussed the details, she kindly thanked me for my time and hoped I would return someday.

"I will come back someday," I answered, with the most sincerity I could manage.

By saying I would be back, it made me feel like I wasn't running out on the women and children I had grown close to over the past several months, the ones who hadn't made it out of the home. I didn't want to say goodbye to Hida either. It would have to be more like a see you later with her. I was tired of losing friends, and we were great roommates.

As I paced around the house, I heard Hida coming home from the university. She came into the kitchen to set her stuff down. I was at the table. My eyes were puffy from crying.

"Hida, I have to go home. "I hope I will be back soon, but my grandma needs me right now."

"Then let's get you a ticket out of here." She was already searching her purse for her travel agency contact in Chicago, another Kosovo-Albanian. She hadn't even blinked when I told her I was leaving, and I was grateful to her for taking over my travel plans.

By the end of the evening, Hida had me set up with a plane ticket and helped me pack. She volunteered to take me to the larger airport in Skopje, Macedonia, but I decided to take a local shuttle near the downtown area to the airport. I hated saying goodbye at airports. It seemed cliché, but I felt all eyes on me in some of the most heart-wrenching moments of my life, all done at the airport.

I made Hida keep what I couldn't carry. She obliged me though I seriously doubted she needed all the junk I had acquired in a place where everything was cheaper than at home. Authentic, no, cheap, yes. I couldn't think about anything except getting home.

"Listen, girl," Hida said as we stood at the shuttle stop at the Ambassador Hotel in downtown Pristina.

When she called me "girl," it made me smile. After all, I was only a few years away from thirty. "You need to be there with your family, but…" She paused, and I could see her face flushed.

She started to tear up, and at the sight of her, I did as well, my eyes already red. "Don't forget about us. We have to make it a point to stay in touch."

It was natural for Hida to consider I would forget about this place. After all, many people did.

"I won't forget, and I know how important it is for us girls to stick together," I said, trying to hold back the memory of another friend who I said I would visit but didn't, until it was too late.

The airport shuttle came with two passengers already in the refurbished minivan. A quick glance at all their luggage and I climbed into the van.

With each bump of the road, my hands came out of my lap, and I gripped the bottom of the plush bench. The houses stood out along the main highway with two lanes of traffic whizzing by. Each one looked somewhat different from another, but the lack of a finished roof united them.

Hida had explained on a previous road trip to Macedonia that to save money on taxes, a homeowner would perpetually live in an unfinished house, thus ensuring less property taxes. What she was unable to explain, or at least I was not able to grasp, was why these same unfinished houses had exquisite marble statues resurrected in the front yards. It was all about appearances.

I dug into my purse for the tenth time, double-checking my passport. I would get my tickets at the counter. For someone so messy, I really valued my obsessive-compulsive rituals. I looked up just in time to see a black Escalade SUV, going way too fast, heading straight for our van.

Crunch.

My seatbelt sliced into my stomach on impact. I fell back hard into the seat and stayed there, stunned from the force of the other vehicle. I looked out the window to see its driver and passenger; two men dressed in black with black ski masks exited the vehicle and got into a small red car that looked like every other car on the road. I was lost in the sequence of events, and somewhere my subconscious gave up the fight to stay awake.

Time stood still for longer than I could remember. Minutes or hours later, I wasn't sure, I felt the strong arms of a military paramedic team wrapped around me.

This was pain. A small sound escaped my lips.

My brain registered the flag on their sleeves was Finnish, and I thought of Maria. I heard my other passengers moaning in pain, and the driver was unconscious. It was hard to see everything from my vantage point, but he looked dead from the look of the metal parts sticking out of his chest.

I was carried outside the van. The motion made me sick, and I threw up. I vaguely remembered the medic turning my neck to save whatever little dignity I still had by not covering my outfit with vomit. He was speaking fast to the other one. I didn't understand. And

I didn't try to. I was a dead weight on the stretcher, weak and vulnerable. I wanted to cry out like a wounded animal, but my throat had closed.

Arguing over the radio, sirens, and people watching. It made me sick. Again. What the fuck were they looking at? Someone had just tried to kill a vanload of people, and they were staring like they were at a parade.

Once the stretcher was loaded into the ambulance, I started to assess how bad it really was. I knew my hands were bleeding, my abdominals felt crushed, but I was alive. The Finnish soldiers seemed calm and confident as they set me up with an oxygen mask. It hurt to breathe on my own, so I welcomed the mask.

One of the men started cutting off my shirt to examine my abdomen. All standard procedure. I had combat lifesaver training and had trained in several medical exercises. It seemed like such a world away. My mind slowed down with the sweet taste of clean air entering my lungs.

I kept replaying the SUV coming toward us repeatedly on the trip to the hospital. Everything else left my brain, and instinctively I felt the stretcher for my weapon. I didn't have a weapon. The Finnish soldiers both had nine-millimeter Berettas attached to the holsters on their hips.

The flash of camouflage brought me back somewhere in my mind. I had trained for but never experienced pain like this. It wasn't so long ago I was crying on a park bench to Gianni about getting deployed and freaking out because I didn't want to face the idea of not coming back a whole person. I didn't want those scars on my life. But who was I kidding? Pain, loss, stress, they could happen anywhere, to anyone, including me. How had I been so fortunate? Crazy lucky that I felt safe enough to fly halfway around the world on my own personal mission and ended up in the back of a Finnish ambulance where no one else in the world would know where I was. I would miss my flight, and I had almost been killed trying to go home. I had to call the police or someone to help me. They needed to call my family.

Two soldiers in familiar uniforms held the doors of the hospital open. I searched their faces for some indication of how bad it was going to be. I wanted to ask questions, but the oxygen mask covered my mouth, and I was at their mercy. Strong hands wheeled me into a bay of machines. I heard English, and I was sure I was in the care of the United States Army.

A tall blonde female sergeant said, "Everything is

going to be okay."

I was relieved to be in the United States camp hospital instead of the one in downtown Pristina. The shame overwhelmed me for those thoughts as I remembered the screams of my fellow passengers. Where were they taken for treatment? When I closed my eyes, I could see the bloodied face of the van driver with glass shattered into his skin. *It's not real. It didn't happen. My mind is tricking me into seeing things that couldn't happen to me or the taxi driver. He had helped me with my baggage only an hour before.* I didn't know, and I couldn't ask. A chill touched my skin as the cold blade of a pair of scissors pressed against my abdomen as the medic cut away the rest of my clothes. The air of the hospital gave me goosebumps on my naked skin, but soon after, the nurse put a sheet over my middle, covering my most sensitive parts from view.

The number of people surrounding my bed grew to nearly ten. All of them working on some part of me. I saw the needles of the IV going in, but I barely felt a stick. I was too focused on the doctor ordering a catheter to monitor my urine for internal bleeding. I repeated, *"It's not real; it couldn't happen,"* with intense focus. IVs and catheters meant something bad was going on.

Hours or minutes later, the staff dwindled down to

two nurses and the doctor, and they finally took off my oxygen mask. I opened my mouth to speak, but the words wouldn't come out. The blonde-haired nurse who had stayed with me since the beginning saw my mouth moving and could see me struggling. She nodded and mouthed. "You are okay."

Chapter Seventeen

"Miss McCoy, slow down," the nurse said. "Can you tell me what you are feeling? The ambulance workers said you complained about your head and your stomach."

The whole ride to the camp was a blur, and I could barely remember mumbling words to the blue-eyed Nordics.

"That's right. But I can't remember much else. Why don't you tell me what's wrong with me?" I managed to say. The sound of my weak voice ran a chill down my spine.

"We have a comedian here." She smiled at my bluntness, and I took my nurse's humor as a good sign.

"That's what we're going to find out. In the meantime, let's not overdo it right now. We need to run some tests and get you fixed up."

"I'm supposed to be on a plane."

"That's okay. We found your passport in your purse," she said. "We already called your family. Your sister is a very sweet girl."

Who was this lady? If I blinked, I would swear she had the wings of an angel, a camouflaged angel, but a gift nonetheless.

"Just relax now, Specialist McCoy. You're in good hands," she said. I believed her. She spoke to me as she tucked the edges of my gown underneath me. I guessed this was for modesty. She shifted my weight the wrong way, and the last thing I remembered thinking before passing out from the pain was how much my family would be worried about me. And the fact that she had called me *specialist*. I wasn't in the Army anymore. At that moment, it was good to hear the title I had earned during my years in the military. Before I felt my bruised ribs underneath my skin, of course.

By the time I woke up, it was nearly a day later and, from the time on the hospital clock, five p.m. I didn't feel the stabbing, sharp pain in my ribs. I felt better, so much better that I wanted to get up and walk around. I couldn't, of course. I had thick bandages around my ribs. I had an IV inserted on the top of my right hand and a little finger clip attached to my index finger. There were tubes filling up a small bag on the side of my bed. Gross.

I glanced around. I wasn't in a private room, but the sliding curtains were pulled closed except for a small opening where I could view the clock and passing nurses. They were not looking at me. They probably already knew I had woken up. If I were them, I'd be curious about a civilian in the camp, who might or might not be important enough to be here.

I watched the IV drip slowly; something good must have been in that bag because I didn't feel a thing. I looked for a call button or something official to get some attention, but not finding anything, I decided on clearing my throat and yelling for a nurse. When in doubt, use whatever means necessary. It wasn't exactly a yell, it ended up more like a howl, more animal-like than human. That was good stuff. Before I could finish, a burly African-American guy pulled back the curtain just enough to slide through.

"Rise and shine. The princess is awake. How do you feel, honey?" He was a soothing baritone.

Okay, seriously, that was way too many questions.

I nodded, but on the chance I might yelp or bark again, I kept my mouth closed.

"We have you on some pretty strong narcotics to help you with the pain, so just try to be still for a while." He explained everything slowly enough for a child, and I could tell he was from the Deep South somewhere, maybe Georgia. He had that Southern drawl that could lull me to sleep in a nice peaceful morphine haze. I motioned to my stomach, hoping he would get my drift. Was I okay?

"You have badly bruised ribs, and that's where your pain comes from, but you really lucked out, ma'am. I'll be back later with your doctor. I am one of your nurses. Once you feel more up to it, the police need to take your statement."

Oh, police. That should hopefully answer the question of why this had happened to me. Did someone try to kill me, or was it the other two in the van? Maybe I was just in the wrong place at the wrong time. I couldn't put the email out of my mind, though, and the threat to me from some unknown person.

Later that night, they decreased my pain medication dosage, and I started to become more lucid. Now the real trouble started, answering questions.

The blonde nurse was back. Jackie Shepherd, her name tag read. She was in scrubs now instead of a uniform. I watched as she warmed up her hands before she checked my vital signs. Jackie seemed like a mothering type, and I was happy she'd found the profession of nursing. It suited her.

A few minutes after Jackie left, a policeman came in escorted by a military police officer from the camp. I wasn't happy to be answering questions, but I was relieved not to be alone with my thoughts. I hadn't decided on the best course of action.

I answered the local policeman's questions, and he didn't seem the least bit surprised about what I said. I guessed he had heard a lot worse than my story about the men in black hitting us and then ditching the vehicle. I wondered about the identity of the other passengers.

"It was a vehicle stolen from one of the local businessmen here," The only explanation he offered as to what had happened to me. "I suggest once you are able, you take the first flight home. You can be on your way very soon."

It was funny that he mentioned going home because even though that was exactly what I wanted to do, he wasn't the first person to tell me to go home; someone else had made that very clear only a few days ago.

Once I answered his questions, I was drained of energy from head to toe. The driver of the van had died on impact, but he wasn't sure if I would be needed for an investigation or a trial. He had word about the passengers and was on his way to question them both.

It was not an accident. I couldn't stay here for any length of time when my own family needed me at home.

After the officer left, Jackie eased the phone underneath my IV tubes and dialed LaLa's cell phone. Jackie was kind, and I silently forgave her for nearly breaking the rest of my ribs before. LaLa answered, and I said hello in my still-raspy voice. Hell, I sounded worse off than I was.

"Jo, can you hear me?"

"Crystal clear, LaLa," I tried to sound sober.

"How are you holding up? Do you want me to come there? I can come right now, just tell me what to do." My mind was racing to catch up to the speed of her voice.

I only had one thing on my mind. "How's Grandma?"

Sometime earlier, I had processed why I was on my way home, and I truly felt helpless. This wasn't a good time to be a victim. My family needed me to be strong.

"Oh, Jo, oh, Jo." And I heard her dropping the

phone. She was sobbing.

My dad's voice came on the line. He was always so stoic and quiet, but he carefully explained that my grandmother was paralyzed on her left side, on a feeding tube, and not speaking yet, but she was alive. "Your mom wants you to come home when you are ready. You just tell me what's best. I can come get you if you need me to."

His voice took me right back home. I needed him. He was the rock underneath our group of McCoy women. He meant what he said, but I had already done enough by being away in the first place. I was used to being around a support system, never alone, or truly alone. But in the past year, I had begun to search out my own adventure, pushing them away for fear that I might suffocate. The thought of my dad leaving the farm to my cousins to come fetch me was just too much for me. I didn't want him to have to come clean up my mess. I had put myself in this situation for better or worse. It was something I told myself during all my military years, to remind myself that I chose to enlist, it was my own fault whatever happened to me.

"No, Dad. I need you to stay put. I can't be there, and I'm sorry, but I will come home soon."

I heard him cough; then he handed the phone to my mom, who kept asking questions I couldn't answer.

Holding the fat beige phone up to my ear was putting a crick in my neck. I didn't like it.

"Listen, Mom, I think my phone card is going to end, so I'd better get off here," I lied, but it worked.

She quickly told me how much she loved me, and I held up the receiver for Jackie to take. I thought of my grandma not speaking—my grandma, she was the best, and there were suddenly so many things I had forgotten to ask her. Sometime later, I drifted off to sleep. I was uncomfortable, but something in my system willed me to rest.

The next morning was full of checkups and visits with the doctors in charge of my case. The tubes were finally coming out except for one. With that, I could shuffle to and from the bathroom with my one IV.

I could feel the bruises every time I tried to lengthen my spine, so I gave up and stayed hunched over. I looked like an old lady with osteoporosis. Very cute, not that I cared too much. I needed a shower and something to wear besides the gown open in the back; my hair needed to be combed. If I was worrying about this, then I must be getting better. Sometime during my yellow and green Jell-O breakfast, washed down with Diet 7UP, I was relieved that I didn't have to see my grandma in a hospital. She was the strong woman who made me proud to be her granddaughter. Her laugh was unforgettable and so much a part of my childhood. I needed her to speak again so I could let her know about Chapa's email.

Being in the painfully white and muted environment made me appreciate my last time with her at her house. Her whole house was full of color: an antique rose-colored chandelier, patchwork quilts, and a massive collection of ceramic chickens, which mirrored the live versions that patrolled her yard. This was the woman I wanted to remember. I smelled nothing here except the salty sweat from being too still for too many days. But in her two-bedroom home, I smelled bacon grease, pancakes, and the wood burning in the indoor stove. Yes, I was lucky to keep her memory there. I would say my goodbye in her home, where she spent her days, not a sterile room where she was oblivious to my presence.

The hobbling trip to the bathroom was enough for one day. I decided this on my way back to the bed.

As I returned to the linen curtain, I heard footsteps inside my cordoned-off area. I pulled back the sheet to see Jackie remaking my bed. She wasn't alone.

I was shocked to see my salsa dance instructor sitting next to my bed. She was smiling and in uniform.

All black like a SWAT team type. But why on Earth would she be here?

Jackie finished the bed and helped me into it. I smiled at my visitor and got comfortable back inside the cocoon of blankets.

"I am so sorry. I just found out," she said in her heavily accented English. It broke the stillness of the room. Jackie turned back and, seeing me relaxed, she closed the curtain. It was a nice gesture her being here, but I honestly couldn't remember my teacher's name.

Her name tag read *Paltrini*. Italian sounding, hmmm. Were there Italians in Argentina? I remembered something about the famous Italian Garibaldi going to South America. Such a weird thought to be having now.

"Thank you for coming, Miss Paltrini," I carefully pronounced her name correctly. "Does my roommate, Hida, know?"

She shifted in her seat and crossed one leg over the other, so ladylike for a police officer. "Oh, yes. She knows, but for security reasons, she wasn't allowed in the camp yet."

"But she's an American," I quipped.

"Yes, but they're just being cautious for now."

"Cautious, so then you heard this may not have been an accident. Well, then, how are you here?"

She thought about this and slowly responded, "I have top security clearance, and I know people. Do you want me to leave?"

Her last question was laced with something I couldn't quite distinguish.

"No, it's fine, I guess. Thanks for coming."

She stared at me for a long while, making me uncomfortable, as if she was trying to make me understand something I could not.

I stared back, a bit unnerved by it all. She glanced at her uniform and looked back at me.

And then I knew. She looked completely different but familiar somehow. I whispered quietly, so only we could hear, "Concepcion Chapa," I was barely audible. "Is it you?"

The name hung in the air around us.

She nodded, and the finality of it all hit me. My eyes were wet tears.

She leaned forward and hugged me close in my hospital bed. Her weight was just below my bruised ribs, but I didn't want her to leave. The pain was palpable, but I couldn't tell her. She kept looking down like she was ashamed.

"Battle buddy, I am so glad you came."

She looked up at me, tears forming in the ducts of her eyes. Light green eyes now like mine, not brown anymore, and a new slender nose.

"Well, I almost didn't." She wiped her eyes with a Kleenex she carefully selected from her pocket stash.

"I'm sorry, I feel like shit. And I look even worse," I tried to silence the thousand questions I wanted to ask, questions I didn't know if she could or should answer. My sanity prevailed. I didn't want to scare her away. She just looked so different. She was already in my life, and I just hadn't recognized her. Her voice carried a heavy accent. That must have taken a lot of practice. After many minutes of watching her fumble with a tissue and look at the floor, I broke the silence.

"So now what do we do?"

She kept her eyes trained on something near the rail on my hospital bed. "We can just sit here for a while." There was no trace of Concepcion in her voice, and for a second I started to consider the woman in front of me as a stranger. But something had lifted minutes before, something internal, and seeing her eyes was believing.

After she said she would stay, I still didn't want to start talking right away. We were in the Army hospital with military personnel, and whoever my friend was before was no more. She was this new person whose identity had to be a secret; too much had changed, tens of thousands of dollars in plastic surgery and more hours of voice training for whatever she was into.

She looked more European than before, less ethnic; it wasn't better looking, just different. Strangely, a little more like me despite the height. From her leg crossed over the other, I could read her tiny boot size on the bottom, four and a half. Well, that settled it.

"How are your salsa routines coming along?" she asked, looking me in the eyes. Her pronunciation of the English words would take some getting used to. Gone was her Boriqua slang, the cutting of the words.

"I think I can do it all solo, but I have to think about it too much," I answered truthfully. "I don't know how it would actually work when I eventually try it with a partner."

"That is the real test," she said slowly like she was thinking about something much more important than my dancing abilities.

"Where did you learn to salsa dance so well?"

The question seemed harmless enough, but I was switching the topic to the subject of her. She didn't take the bait. We both knew she had learned as a kid and in fact, had tried to teach me in our recreation area countless times while in the Army together.

"Oh, you know, here and there. It's in my blood."

Yes, her supposedly Italian-Argentinian blood. I thought of Gianni and what his reaction would be to his old friend's transformation, and what about her ex-fiancé, whose heart she broke?

What would they say about this? They had devoted so much energy to finding her, and she was alive and more elusive than we'd considered.

"How is your family?" Finally, she asked me a real question.

My family loved her. She had never seemed jealous when I had received more packages and mail than her on our deployment. She always gave me advice on how to handle all the drama that came along with having two sisters and a nosy mom.

"My family is good; my mom is worried because I'm here, and I'm sure my dad is keeping her from jumping on the next plane. LaLa is still working in St. Louis with the police. Emma had another girl, so now I have two beautiful nieces, Chelsea and Zoey. I mean, not much has changed back home."

She nodded. "Are they still trying to figure out how to get you married?"

Her question made me think about my grandma, and I willed myself to come back to the present. I had a chance to speak to Concepcion again, and I wasn't going to waste it.

For the first time, I heard her training slipping. It wasn't her accent but the way she arranged the question. She sounded like a native speaker.

We eased into our conversation, no longer timid. We gossiped for over an hour. Back and forth we talked about nothing, but it reminded me of what it was like to have the familiarity back with a friend; some part of her had been like family. I started to feel the numbing pain of my muscles from lying in the bed and looking over at the now Paltrini. I shifted as much as I could.

As fast as she appeared back into my life, Concepcion was gone after a quick formal goodbye.

When she leaned to kiss my cheek, she whispered in my ear for only me to hear. "I've got your back, Jo," she said as I closed my eyes to focus on her words. "I love you. It's not safe for me to see anyone now, but maybe soon."

"Love you, girl," I said, because it was the only thing I wished I had said before. "If I ever get married, you have to come."

She laughed. "Love you, too. We'll have to see what happens. I don't see a ring on your finger yet," She wiped her eyes.

I looked at her, the eyes of a stranger and of my best friend in the whole world. I saw the faint circle of a contact lens, no doubt a colored one. Here she was again, back from the grave, protecting me from all the bad, just like she had for so many years. I couldn't deny I needed her.

We put on a good show at the end just in case the nurses outside were paying attention. I was alone again in the bed, and I fought back the sadness. We could never be friends like before, but at least she was still alive and choosing to be someone else. I didn't know why she came back or what would happen. But for the first time, I really wanted to go home.

Chapter Eighteen

"You are seriously letting me walk out of here?" I asked the black male nurse, Andre, who was Jackie's replacement. "I am still walking like the hunchback of Notre Dame."

"With an attitude like that, how did you ever survive in the military?" Andre quipped. "You're supposed to be a soldier, girl. You'd better lock it up and save all that complaining about your seatmate. You're flying home today."

Flying home sounded great, but a day-long plane trip in my condition was going to be hell. I sat up in bed and combed my tangled strands of hair in the small handheld mirror Andre found for me.

"What kind of painkillers are you giving me for the plane ride?" I had to be sensible. My middle section was one large marbled bruise.

"We're going to get you set up nice," Andre said. "You are even booked in the first-class section on Lufthansa Airlines."

First class sounded great, but Lufthansa Airlines was my last choice for international flights. Not after I had been stuck for ten hours trying to convince myself to just eat the nasty sausage thing they served for dinner. I had lost three pounds on that flight.

"Well, next time ask before you spend my money on something like first-class tickets."

He didn't answer.

After I finished applying some of the makeup Jackie left for me, Andre brought in another female soldier to help me dress. The young private was embarrassed about the whole ordeal. I was done feeling shy after being in the hospital and the catheter experiment.

"You are so lucky to be going home," she draped my blouse over my shoulders.

I considered keeping my mouth shut, but all veterans have an urgent need to tell the younger generation of soldiers just how lucky they are.

"Kosovo isn't so bad," I said. "At least you're here

on a peacekeeping mission."

She buttoned my blouse while I hung on to the rail on the side of my bed. I silently prayed those pain pills would do the trick. I couldn't even dress myself. How was I going to recover on my own?

"My boyfriend is over in Afghanistan," she continued. "I wish I could be with him."

I was glad she wasn't. Female soldiers in Afghanistan had some of the worst living conditions. How could the women have their normal monthly cycles camped on a mountain ridge for three months? No showers for the boys, fine. It wasn't the same for us.

"If he's any good, then he will wait for you," I said. "Instead of moping around, you have to make the most of your time apart. Take some college classes here, play beach volleyball, hang out at the coffee bar, and read. It'll go by faster than you think."

She stayed quiet for the rest of my getting dressed.

"You are ready to go now," she said. "I will let the nurse know. Have a safe trip."

I maneuvered on to the bed to save Andre the trouble.

"Are you decent, Miss McCoy?" Andre said from outside the curtain. "I have a male escort here for your journey."

Male escort? How much of my money was Andre

spending? I wasn't paying for two first-class sausage dinners, that was for sure.

"I'm dressed," I said. "Show me Mr. Wonderful."

Andre pulled back the curtain, slowly revealing my prize. "Here's Gianni," he said, with an introduction meant for the late-night host Johnny Carson. He winked and thankfully gave us some privacy.

"Hi, Joelle," Gianni said, crossing the distance between us in three large steps. "I came as soon as I heard. I thought I was going to lose you again."

"You almost did," I answered solemnly. I touched the back of his hand. "I am glad you came. I look like crap, but I think I'm going to make it."

"*We* will make it," he said, emphasizing the word *we*. "I'm going home with you. If you'll let me, I want to help get you back on your feet."

"Who told you where I was?"

"It sounds too good to be true, but I think it was Agent Chapa," he said. "I got a text that I needed to call your sister. It was an anonymous number. I called LaLa, and she told me about the accident. She didn't send the original text, though. I just can't think of any other explanation."

"She was here, Gianni," I said. "She's alive, and she risked everything to see me. She is alive and living her life."

I teared up, remembering our short visit together. I was lucky to have a friend like her. I was more alive somehow too.

Gianni wiped my tears away with his finger. His eyes were wet, too. I could tell he loved her in his own way.

"She is tough as nails. But then again, so are you."

"Let's go home, Gianni."

"Sounds like a plan," he responded. "I booked us in first class so you can sleep all of this off."

Gianni looked like he needed a good nap, too. I doubted he slept since he'd found out. He helped me off the bed, and we walked to check out.

"My only request is that we pick up some edible food before we fly on a German airline."

"Done," he said. "I didn't know you were such an airline expert."

"It doesn't take an expert, just one long flight from hell. Next time, I pick the airline."

CPSIA information can be obtained
at www.ICGtesting.com
Printed in the USA
FFHW011204060619
52849758-58398FF

9 781633 633841